EX·LIB 6 —

Bowman of Crécy

RONALD WELCH

Bowman of Crécy

ILLUSTRATED BY IAN RIBBONS

CRITERION BOOKS
NEW YORK

Library of Congress Catalog Card Number 67-17485
This book was published in Great Britain in 1966
under the same title by Oxford University Press

Manufactured in the United States of America

Other books by Ronald Welch

Escape from France

For the King

Nicholas Carey

Contents

GLOSSARY

ARMOUR:
Bascinet. 14th Century Helmet, basin shaped with hinged visor in front, and with a hood of mail attached (Camail) to cover the throat and neck.

Brassart. Vambrace. Jambart. Steel plates strapped over the upper arm, lower arm, and legs.

Brigandine. Armour of footmen and bowmen. Short leather or canvas coat with steel plates riveted on the outside.

Mace. Armour-smashing weapon. Short, heavy handle with large steel ball at the end.

COSTUME:
Cotehardie. Short, close fitting tunic, buttoned at front.

Gambeson. Padded, quilt-like garment worn under armour to protect the skin against bruises or chafing from mail or steel plates.

Surcoat or Surcote. Long garment worn *either* over armour as protection against sun or possibly rain, too, as rust was a great enemy of armour.
Or. Worn over ordinary clothes. Gave way to the cotehardie.

Jupon. Another form of surcoat, worn over armour and embroidered with arms of the wearer.

CASTLES:
The *Keep* was a round or square tower built on top of a mound. It was the last line of defence. The first and outer line was a wall with towers at intervals and a gatehouse. The space between this wall and the Keep was the *Ward* or the *Bailey.* A V-shaped ditch was dug round the foot of the mound and the walls.

Bowman of Crécy

I

AMBROSE OF BEVERLEY

The three men moved quickly and silently through the forest. They were almost invisible in the dark shadows where the trees grew thickest, and when they came out into the open and the bright sunlight to cross some clearing, their dark-green jerkins and hose merged with the background of bush and leaf. They were all armed with a sword and dagger, and each carried a great bow, five feet or more of polished wood.

The man in the lead stopped abruptly and held up his hand. The other two halted like well-trained hounds.

'What is it, Hugh?'

'Someone shouting, Nick.'

Nick was little more than a boy, short and stocky, with a brown face and an upturned, inquisitive nose. His ears stood out almost comically on each side of his head as he listened intently.

'Did you hear it, Jack?' Hugh asked.

Jack spat and shook his head. He was the oldest of the three, a battered veteran, his hair and beard streaked with grey, his face seamed and wrinkled like a piece of old leather, and much the same colour. The chalky-white line of an old wound ran across his forehead, and his nose was mis-shapen, broken in some fight long ago.

'Can't hear anything, Hugh,' he said.

'It was to the north. On the road. Nick, keep on my left. Jack, to the right. Don't loose unless I do.'

He pulled out a shaft from the quiver on his back, and the others did the same. They moved on again, watching Hugh, and following the line that he was taking. Neither had questioned his orders. Jack was a master bowman and a veteran of several campaigns, but he had spent five years only in the forest, and he could never acquire Hugh's instinctive sense of sound or direction in the tangle of trees and glades where a stranger would have lost himself within a matter of minutes. As for Nick, he had lived in the forest for most of his life, like Hugh, but he followed Hugh in everything that he did with the devotion of a puppy obeying his master.

The trees thinned out, and ahead lay the road that skirted the northern edge of the forest of Goodrich. They could all hear shouts now, and the unmistakable clatter of hooves on the hard surface of the road.

'To the left!' Hugh shouted, and began to run.

The road swung to the right and then up a gradual slope. On the left was a wide glade running away into the depths of the forest, and Hugh halted there, glancing down at his shaft as he put it to the string. It had a broad head, the kind he used for hunting, with three feathers that he had trimmed himself, two of them grey, and the third, the cock feather, brightly coloured, and glued at right angles to the groove cut in the heel of the shaft, so that a bowman could nock without any delay.

'I bet you three of my best shafts that it's Walter,' he said.

'Very likely,' Jack said, and spat. His voice was hoarse, the result, he had once told Hugh, of looted wine in Normandy, and he spat frequently as a matter of habit. Hugh often thought that he could interpret Jack's moods by the sound of his spitting; this was one of disgust.

Six men suddenly appeared at the top of the slope and rushed down the road, looking back over their shoulders. Four of them carried swords, and the others had bows. They saw the glade and swerved towards it as four horsemen with steel helmets and mail shirts swept over the hill and galloped furiously down the slope, shouting and waving swords.

'That's Walter!' Nick cried.

'Draw!' Hugh shouted. 'Aim for the horses!'

He brought up his bow, drawing steadily as he did so, the string pulling back the thick limbs of the bow, until his right hand was at his ear, his left hand clamped like a vice on the grip, and the knuckles on a level with the leading horseman. Gradually he relaxed the grip of his fingers on the string. The shaft hissed away, rising slightly and then swooping down. But Hugh had not paused to watch the flight; he had nocked the next shaft and was drawing again. As he came up to the aim, he saw three horses rearing up and their riders trying to control them. The fourth man galloped on, huddling down in his saddle. As Hugh loosed at him he heard Jack and Nick's bows twang and watched the three shafts. One whistled over the man's head as he ducked; the other two caught his wretched horse full in the chest. The animal swerved violently and flung its rider to the ground.

'Run!' Hugh shouted, and turned to make for the shelter of the trees. They did not stop until they had covered nearly a mile and were deep in the forest. Though they had run for most of the way, they were still breathing easily as Hugh sat down on a fallen tree-trunk and scowled angrily.

He was a formidable looking young man, over six feet in height, and very powerfully built. His fair hair, bleached by the sun, hung nearly to his shoulders; a curving, arrogant nose and pointed chin gave his dark-brown face an expression of great resolution.

'The fools!' he said. 'Did you see them, Jack? Running straight down an open glade, where those horsemen would have caught them before they had gone a hundred paces!'

'Walter's a townsman,' Jack said.

'I wish he'd go back there. We should have kept our shafts and left Walter.'

'You couldn't do that, Hugh,' Jack said. 'Those were Sir Henry Mortimer's men. I saw his coat of arms on their surcoats. You know what he'd have done to Walter if he'd caught him.' He spat vigorously. 'He'd have died slow.'

'His own fault then,' Hugh said impatiently. 'Now he'll bring Sir Henry and his men scouring the forest for us. We've got to get rid of Walter.'

'I'm with you!' Nick said instantly, his freckled face twitching with excitement.

'So am I!' Jack said. 'But he's got friends in the camp, Hugh. And Geoffrey's too sick to help.'

'I know, I know!' Hugh said angrily. 'Well, we came out for deer, so we'll try to the west.'

They moved off again in single file, with Hugh, as usual, in the lead, and covered another mile before he stopped once more, head up, and sniffing.

'Fire,' he said, 'and someone roasting meat.'

Out came three shafts, and they walked slowly forward, eyes on the ground so that their soft leather boots would not tread on a twig or a piece of dry wood. They did not know what lay ahead, but anything strange in the forest might be dangerous. Hugh held up his hand, and they waited while he crept towards an old and twisted oak-tree, and cautiously put his head round the trunk. Long ago he had been taught never to rush out recklessly from cover, and to observe his quarry before he made a move.

But nothing could have been more peaceful or harmless than the scene before him now. Below was a wide hollow, quite clear of trees, and warm and quiet in the sunlight. Blue smoke drifted over the turf from a fire on the farther side, and squatting beside it was a man, turning a spit on which he had impaled a rabbit. Behind him were tethered a horse and a mule.

Jack's tongue licked his lips as he smelt the roasting meat, and Nick grinned with delight. But they still waited for Hugh to make the first move. He looked around the hollow, but there was no one else there. As for the man himself, he did not look particularly dangerous. He carried no weapons, and his cotehardie and hose were of good quality. He was short and plump, with a round, red face and a shining bald scalp. He hummed cheerfully as he turned the spit, and then bent down to sniff the meat.

Hugh nocked a shaft, and drew, though not to the ear. The shaft flickered lazily across the hollow and hit the tree by the fire with a solid clunk. The fat little man jumped to his feet with a high-pitched cry. He stared at the shaft and the feathers which were still quivering from the impact, and then turned quickly as the three men came out of the trees and walked towards him. His sharp, twinkling eyes went from one brown face to the other, and he kept his hands away from his sides. One glance at those great bows and the dress of the men was enough. He knew who and what these men were who had emerged so silently from the depths of the forest.

'Who are you?' Hugh asked curtly.

'I am Ambrose of Beverley, young sir. A doctor. A most skilled doctor.'

'A quack, you mean. Peddling coloured water by the roadside.'

'Indeed not, sir,' Ambrose said indignantly, drawing himself up to his full height, though still dwarfed by Hugh's tall figure. His eyes twinkled. 'Laudat venales qui vult extradere merces,' he added.

'And what does that mean?'

'A man must praise those wares which he wishes to sell.'

Hugh smiled, a surprisingly pleasant smile from that hard and determined face, and Ambrose looked at him with a fresh interest.

'Well, you're honest enough,' Hugh said. 'What are you doing in the forest?'

Ambrose sighed. 'The food at the inn last night!' he said, rolling up his eyes in horror. 'It would not have satisfied the fleas that filled the place. And as you can see, young sir, I have much to fill,' and he patted his round stomach.

'That rabbit will fill me,' Jack said. 'Just done, too.'

'Pray help yourself,' Ambrose said instantly. 'And I have some good wine here, too.'

He bustled about, but his eyes were wistful as he watched Jack tear the roast meat into pieces. Hugh handed him some, and his good humour returned immediately. He poured out the wine and squatted by the fire, eating and chattering incessantly. He was an entertaining talker, with his stories of the different people he met on his travels, gossip from London, and the latest news about King Edward's last campaign in France. Jack listened eagerly to this, for the King, the third Edward of his name, was already a famous soldier, and Jack had served under him in Normandy.

Hugh said nothing. He ate and drank, and scowled at the fire, breaking in abruptly on one of Ambrose's stories.

'Are you really a good doctor?' he asked.

'I am,' Ambrose smiled. 'But you do not need my help. I can see that.'

'I have a friend who does.'

'Geoffrey!' Nick exclaimed.

'Yes. Geoffrey. You will come with us, Ambrose.'

'Of course, sir, of course!' Ambrose jumped to his feet. He had no choice, but he showed no sign of fear, Hugh noticed.

'For your sake, I hope you are a good doctor,' he said.

'What ails your friend?'

'An arrow wound. In the shoulder.'

Ambrose nodded, and his face was calm and confident. A wound was often a straightforward matter, and he could deal with wounds. But a lingering illness of the body was something that no honest doctor could treat with confidence, and Ambrose was honest and skilled enough to be aware of the limits of his craft.

He saddled his horse, while Nick and Jack carefully stamped

out the embers of the fire. There had been no rain for several weeks, and they had learnt from bitter experience the dangers of a forest fire.

'Nick, lead the mule,' Hugh said curtly. 'Jack, stay in the rear. You, Ambrose, follow me, and don't try to ride away.' He tapped the dark wood of his great bow, and stalked away towards the trees.

Ambrose twitched his reins. He had no intention of kicking his horse into a gallop with the hope of vanishing into the shelter of the forest. He would have been lost in any case, but he knew what a long-bow could do, and these men were probably master bowmen. Before he could have ridden twenty paces three cloth-yard shafts would have been driven through his back; his plump little body shuddered at the thought.

They moved on in silence, and Ambrose soon recovered his normal cheerfulness. He was a man of insatiable curiosity with a deep interest in people, for human beings and their troubles were his livelihood. These outlaws were a fresh experience for him, and he observed them now closely as he rode under the trees and along the narrow, winding tracks through the dense forest.

It was the young man whom they called Hugh, who interested him most. Jack was an old bowman, a type that Ambrose had often met on the roads, and Nick was young and not very intelligent, he guessed. But Hugh was an unusual young man, Ambrose decided. A formidable looking person, with his aloof, and almost ruthless expression of grim resolution. Intelligent, too, and a natural leader, and yet there was that one charming smile that the doctor had noticed. He wished to learn more about this unusual outlaw.

After half an hour Ambrose had lost all sense of direction. Hugh did not seem to follow any particular track, though he never hesitated. Once they crossed an open stretch of moorland, and in the far distance Ambrose saw the blue, hazy outlines of mountains, near the Marches of Wales, he guessed. Then suddenly they plunged once more into the gloom of the forest, and Ambrose looked about uneasily. He loved the sun and the wide sweeps of the open road, and he disliked this dark and unknown world that seemed to close in upon him.

Hugh turned to follow the line of a little stream, and they came out into a wide clearing. Small, ill-built huts of wattle and daub were scattered about, smoke drifted across from several fires around which sat men and women, and some children were playing by the stream. It was a dirty and squalid scene, and Ambrose's sharp, inquisitive nose twitched with disgust.

Hugh halted by a hut that was larger and better built than any of the others, and Ambrose dismounted and followed him inside. The furniture was crude, some stools, a chest, and a table, but the place was surprisingly clean and tidy compared to the squalor and filth outside.

'There,' Hugh said, and pointed to a man lying on a truckle-bed.

Ambrose bent over his patient, a man of enormous size, who was tossing restlessly, and groaning in his sleep.

'I can see nothing here,' Ambrose said. 'You will have to carry him outside.'

Jack and Hugh did so, but with some difficulty, and they put the bed down on the grass outside the hut. Ambrose unwound the bandages over the man's shoulder, clean bandages, he noticed, and the puckered wound beneath was clean, too, but the skin was red and inflamed. He pressed it gently and the man winced at the slightest touch of the doctor's plump fingers.

'An arrow, you say?' Ambrose said, looking up at Hugh, who was watching him with an anxious expression. 'There is still some of the head in the wound, I think.'

Jack spat angrily. 'I cut it out myself,' he said. 'I've dealt with plenty of arrow wounds in my life. He's a quack, Hugh!'

Hugh shook his head. 'I think he's right, Jack. Can you find it, Ambrose?'

'I can but try, Master Hugh. Bring me that saddle-bag from the mule.'

He laid out his instruments on a cloth while Hugh watched him. The forest might have been Hugh's home all his life, and his knowledge of the outside world almost worthless, but he knew a craftsman when he saw him at work. Geoffrey was watching, too, and lying there in the open, he seemed even larger and longer of leg than he had appeared in the dark hut.

'To your work, torturer,' he muttered.

'Yes, it will be painful,' Ambrose said.

Five long minutes later he sighed and held up a small piece of metal.

'As small as that,' Geoffrey said faintly. 'It felt the size of a helmet.' His dark hair and beard were streaming as if someone had thrown a bucket of water over his head. Hugh knelt down and held a leather mug of wine to his lips, while Ambrose watched and smiled as he saw the expression of deep concern on that determined face.

When he had smeared the wound with ointment and replaced the bandages, he sat at the table in the hut, and one of the women of the camp brought some food.

'Who is your friend?' Ambrose asked Hugh.

'He is called Geoffrey of Cambridge. He was once a scholar, and killed a man in a tavern brawl. So he came to the forest.'

'When was that?'

'Ten years ago, perhaps more. I have forgotten.'

'And you, Master Hugh?'

Hugh scowled, and the hard, wary expression returned to his face.

'You ask too many questions, Ambrose. We don't like them here.'

Ambrose shrugged his plump shoulders. 'I am a curious man,' he said. 'What harm can I do you by asking questions?'

Hugh's face cleared and he smiled, for he had taken a liking to this cheerful little man.

'I am called Hugh,' he said. 'Some call me Hugh Fletcher because I have some skill in making shafts.'

'And how did you come to the forest?'

'I have always been here. One of the older men told me once that my father and mother were found by the roadside, dying of the plague. The outlaws brought me with them. I was a baby then.'

'And who were your parents, Master Hugh?'

Hugh frowned. 'I don't know, and I don't care. I have made my own way, and I always shall.'

Ambrose inspected the strong chin and smiled. This young man, brought up in the freedom of life in the forest, without restraint or discipline, had been taught to take by force whatever he needed. He would go far, the little doctor decided.

'But you are not altogether happy in this life of yours, are you?' he asked.

Hugh glared at him angrily. 'Why do you say that?' he demanded.

'It is not difficult to see that, Master Hugh. You are a great deal more intelligent than most of your friends, I think.'

Hugh brought his clenched fist down on the table. 'They are not all my friends!' he said. 'Half of them are murderers and thieves.'

'But all outlaws are criminals, surely?'

Hugh's sudden burst of anger had vanished. 'You know little about outlaws, Ambrose,' he said. 'Many of the men here ran away because of some trouble with their lord, or because of debts, or just because they had no work. All they want is to be allowed to live quietly in the forest.' He stared at the table. 'And that is what I am going to give them,' he added.

Ambrose put his hand to his mouth to hide a smile. It was clear to him that the outlaws were going to be given just that by this determined young man whether they wanted it or not.

Hugh looked up as they heard shouts from outside. He jumped to his feet.

'A fight,' he said impatiently. 'They're always fighting. That's one of the things I want to change.'

Ambrose followed him out of the hut. Two men were rolling over and over on the grass, snarling at each other like a pair of dogs. Both had daggers, Ambrose noticed, and he saw one arm go up, and then the broad, sharply pointed blade came down with a vicious jerk. There was a scream of agony, and one man stood up, wiping the sweat from his face, and panting like a hound that had just run down its quarry. But the other man lay on the ground, and did not move.

'Who was that?' Hugh asked Jack. The old bowman was sitting placidly on a stool, watching the murderous little scene with complete composure.

'Will Miller,' he said. He spat, as if in a last salute to the unfortunate Will. 'He and Robert had an argument about their share of what they took from some pedlars this morning. Robert knifed him.'

Hugh clenched his fists. 'The fools!' he said.

Jack turned and looked at Hugh for a long moment, and then he stood, one brown fist touching his sword-hilt and then his dagger.

'There's only one way to stop it, Hugh,' he said. 'And that's to have it out with Walter. I'll come with you.'

'No!' Hugh drew a deep breath. 'I must do this myself, Jack.'

Jack nodded. 'Watch him, Hugh. He's a dirty fighter. He'll stab you in the back if he can.'

Hugh walked down towards the group by the fire, and all the men there fell silent as they saw the expression on his face.

'What's this, Walter?' Hugh asked quietly.

'Just a little argument, Master Hugh.' Walter smiled, but his eyes were wary and suspicious. He was a foot shorter than Hugh, but his arms were long, quite out of proportion to his height, and he had wide shoulders and a barrel of a chest. His black hair and beard were long and untidy, and his clothes were in keeping with his general appearance—faded, patched, and filthy. He seldom looked a man in the face for more than a

second, and then his bloodshot eyes shifted away uneasily. Hugh detested and despised him as a stupid and violent man, but he knew him to be dangerous, capable of murdering another man without the slightest compunction, and with a considerable amount of pleasure.

'Jack tells me that it was you and young Nick who shot down those men of Sir Henry's this morning,' he said.

'You needn't thank me,' Hugh said curtly. 'If I'd had my way, I'd have left you to fend for yourself.'

Walter's eyes flickered, and he stiffened. The other men drew back, and a dead silence fell on the group. Hugh heard Jack's loud spit and an excited whimper from Nick.

'That is very unfriendly of you, Master Hugh,' Walter said. He spoke quietly enough; he was not afraid of a fight, but he had discovered that a cold and menacing politeness was extremely effective. It was wasted, though, on Hugh.

'Those were Sir Henry Mortimer's men after you,' Hugh said. 'You know him, and if you don't, we all do here. He'll scour the forest for us now.'

'What of it? The forest's big enough.'

'He'll find us. And what can we do? No defences, no leader, no sentries to warn us. We'll be cut to pieces, or end by hanging over the walls of Goodrich Castle.'

A muttered growl of agreement went round the group of outlaws, and Walter glared at them angrily.

'What do you suggest then?' he asked Hugh.

'I would move to another and safer place I know of. And then see that we keep off the roads.'

'What should we live on? Acorns and nuts? We brought in some good money today. What have you ever fetched that was any use?'

'I bring in the deer you all eat.'

There was another hum of agreement. Walter's eyes flickered from side to side, and Hugh watched him intently. The moment was coming, he knew, when the talking would end. Walter did not hesitate. He knew, too, that a fight, and death for one of them, was the only possible end to this quarrel. It had been simmering for some weeks, but no one had forced him to a fight yet. He was not a great swordsman, but he was quick, and his greatest advantage lay in his enormous reach.

'I'm tired of you, Master Hugh,' he said. 'A mangy little puppy telling his master what to do.'

Hugh smiled. 'Then I'll tell you again,' he said. 'If you're not out of the forest within the hour, I'll throw you out.'

Walter paused for a moment, his eyes for once fixed, as he tried to make a last estimate of this young man. He did not like what he saw now, but he was no coward, and he had been drinking. He snatched the dagger from his belt with the left hand, and drew his sword, standing there on the balls of his feet, knees slightly bent. The evening sun flashed on the wide blade as he brought up the sword, and his tongue passed slowly over his lips.

2

THE ATTACK ON THE CAMP

Hugh stepped back. He kept his eyes on Walter as he drew sword and dagger. He had seen him once in a fight that had never begun, for Walter had stabbed his opponent as the other was drawing a sword. Hugh felt his heart pounding, and his stomach was empty. He knew the signs. They meant fear, the fear he had known as a boy before a beating, before his first fight, and the first time he had stood and loosed at a man when the outlaws had been attacked in the forest.

His fingers shifted on the sword-grip as Walter moved to the right. They circled warily around each other with slow, deliberate strides, almost daintily like dancers in some masque, an odd sight for two men who were trying to kill each other. But neither wore a helmet or a mail shirt. Either of those swords would end the business with one hard lunge, and a mere wound would not end the fight. The dagger would finish what the sword had not done.

Around they went again, and Hugh smiled grimly. Walter was trying to manœuvre him into a position where the sun would shine in his eyes. Even the slightest hesitation would be fatal. Hugh jumped to the right, sword raised. Walter spun round, and for a moment they stood still. Hugh waited. He had been taught by Jack and Geoffrey how to use a sword, but speed and balance were the vital lessons he had learnt. You could cut and thrust with these broad-bladed swords, but when a man wore no armour the quick thrust would win the fight, and Walter, with his longer reach, had the advantage there. He would wait for him, Hugh decided, and he watched those bloodshot eyes, half closed now, mere slits in the bearded face, the mouth open to show the white teeth. Like a wild boar in the forest, Hugh thought, and as merciless.

The eyes flickered. Walter slid his right foot forward and lunged. Hugh jumped. The long blade flashed past him, and he swept down at the outstretched arm. But Walter wriggled away and Hugh's blade hissed over his arm. A mutter went round the circle of watching men, and they shifted from one foot to the other. Hugh flexed his fingers on the hilt. He had been gripping too tightly he realized.

Walter lunged again. Hugh brought his sword across and the two blades screeched as they met. Walter stepped back and hacked down at Hugh's wrist, but he was too late. He snarled and thrust low as Hugh leapt back. Once more they circled round, both panting with the tension rather than their exertions. Walter started to lunge, and Hugh's sword came across instinctively. The lunge changed to a sweep, and desperately Hugh tried to step back. He felt a sharp, burning streak of pain across his right thigh.

A shout went up from the outlaws, and then they fell silent. Hugh dared not look down. It was only a deep scratch, he thought. Another couple of inches and his leg would have been slashed to the bone, leaving him helpless on the ground. He saw a brief and frightening picture of Walter standing over him, stabbing down mercilessly at his writhing figure.

He drew a deep breath and tried to relax his grip on his sword-hilt. His whole body was burning with heat and his face was wet with sweat. Warm blood was trickling down his leg, and he wondered if that cut was deeper than he had thought. If so, he could not last much longer. He could not wait for Walter to attack now, and he jumped forward, right arm out at full stretch. But Walter scuttled back, moving with an ungainly speed, and again the blades clashed as he parried the thrust. He swerved to one side, and cut across; Hugh ducked and the sword whistled over his head. He thrust again—and before Walter had recovered his balance. The sword jarred in Hugh's hand; he heard a yell from Walter and the shouts of the outlaws. Walter was shuffling to the left, a ragged tear on the right sleeve of his leather jerkin, and the blood was trickling down his arm.

'Finish him, boy!' a hoarse voice cried.

Hugh leapt forward, sword raised for a cut at Walter's head. Up went the other's guard, and Hugh changed the slash to a thrust, right foot sliding over the smooth turf, and drove the point through Walter's chest. His knees gave way, his sword and dagger dropped from his hands, and he crumpled up on the ground, and then turned slowly over on his back.

'Cut his throat, Hugh,' Jack said.

Hugh shook his head. He had fought before in the camp, but he had never followed the usual custom among the outlaws. They never allowed a beaten enemy any mercy; if he was wounded, they finished him with the dagger.

Jack looked down at Walter, and turned away with grim satifaction.

'No need,' he said.

Hugh wiped the sweat from his forehead. His hands, he noticed angrily, were shaking, as he pushed his way through the outlaws, and he did not listen to Nick's excited chatter. He sat down on the stool outside the hut, and Ambrose bent down to look at his leg.

'Let me see that cut, Master Hugh,' he said.

Ambrose left the camp two days later. By that time Geoffrey's wound was healing quickly, and the little doctor said that there was nothing more he could do for him. Hugh and Nick guided

him to the edge of the forest, and waved as Ambrose trotted down the road, before they turned and vanished into the forest once more.

Hugh walked slowly and in a thoughtful silence, and Nick, seeing his mood, for once kept quiet. A decisive moment had come for him, Hugh was thinking. Now that he had killed Walter, the majority of the outlaws would follow his lead, and Hugh was quite clear in his mind what that lead would be. He knew of a secluded valley in the forest, one that could be defended easily, though he hoped that, if his plans were carried out, there would be little need for defence. Most of the men wanted to be left alone, and if they kept off the roads and highway robbery the local authorities around the forest would probably leave them alone. He would start when he reached the camp, Hugh decided. If anyone argued with him. . . . He clenched his hands and thrust out his strong chin. There would be no argument; he would see to that.

Nick had stopped, and Hugh bumped into him.

'What is it, Nick?'

'Wood smoke. A fire!'

Hugh came back to the world of the forest. He sniffed, and then began to run, and for once he did not care how much noise he made as he crashed through the undergrowth, ducked beneath branches, swerved violently around trees, and leapt over occasional streams. He went so fast that he left Nick trailing behind, and he did not stop until he reached a long ridge from where it was possible to look over the forest towards the south. He clambered up into the lower branches of a tree, and Nick, panting desperately, joined him there.

A cloud of black smoke was drifting slowly over the trees, and Nick glanced fearfully at Hugh. That ominous smoke came from the direction of the camp.

'Sir Henry Mortimer!' Nick exclaimed.

Hugh said nothing. He dropped down to the ground and began to run again, through the tangle of trees and clearings, keeping instinctively to the line that would lead him directly to the camp. He was, he thought, about half a mile away when he heard voices. He held up his hand in warning, and both of them dropped flat on their faces. Hugh pulled out a shaft from his quiver, and went forward on hands and knees until he lay behind a fallen tree-trunk. Cautiously he raised his head until he could see into a little clearing just ahead. Women and children were sitting there on the grass, and he recognized them, and the men, too, about thirty in all, standing in groups, dejected and weary by the look of them, Hugh guessed.

They were holding bows, and he knew better than to walk forward towards them without some warning. They would loose at him immediately they saw a figure emerge from the trees. He lay on his back, put his hands to his mouth, and called with the hunting-cry that he often used.

'Who's that?' a man called.

'Hugh. Hugh Fletcher!'

He stood up and walked into the clearing, to be surrounded by a shouting and confused crowd of outlaws, each man trying to tell him what had happened.

'Quiet!' Hugh shouted. He pointed to one whom he knew to be the most intelligent and coherent man there. 'You, Will!'

The story was one he had expected to hear. Sir Henry Mortimer had fallen upon the camp without warning, and with him about twenty bowmen and a dozen mounted men-at-arms. There had been some villeins from his manor, too, Will thought, but they had done little fighting, and had probably come very unwillingly. Sir Henry was a hard and ruthless lord, and not a single one of his tenants would have raised a finger to help him if they could avoid doing so.

As soon as the attack had started, the foresters and bowmen among the outlaws had scattered into the shelter of the woods. The townsmen, mostly friends of Walter, had been cut down, and then Sir Henry had set fire to the huts, and ridden away.

'Geoffrey?' Hugh asked anxiously. 'What happened to Geoffrey?'

'He is over there under the tree, Hugh. He could run a little, and we helped him.'

'And the horses?' These were Hugh's main interest in the camp, for he had built up quite a large stable, to sell them in the nearest towns.

'They didn't find them, Hugh. They were in the caves.'

It could have been worse, Hugh thought. Indeed, all this

would make it much easier for him to carry out his plans. Then suddenly he realized that there was one familiar face missing, and he could see by the shuffling feet and troubled expressions that his fears were right.

'Jack!' he shouted. 'Where's Jack?'

They shook their heads. They knew that Geoffrey, Nick, and Jack Cherryman were Hugh's closest friends. Hugh seized Will's arm and shook it angrily.

'What happened to Jack? Tell me, man!'

'They took him prisoner, Hugh. They got Roger Smith, too.'

They looked at him uneasily, shame-faced and nervous, for this was something that Hugh had so often warned them might happen. Hugh clenched his hands, and he scowled at them with such an expression of suppressed fury that they avoided his glance.

Sir Henry held the fief of Goodrich on the north of the forest. Hugh had seen him several times, the last a few weeks ago in the little town of Skenfrith where he had gone to sell three horses, and he had looked up to see a tall and slender man riding past, with a pale, calm face, a neatly trimmed beard, and brown hair. Everything about him reflected the same sense of tidiness, the cotehardie and the mantle of scarlet, and his carefully groomed horse.

He had stopped close by Hugh to purchase something at one of the stalls, speaking quietly and even courteously, and when he had finished, he gave his orders to the men-at-arms behind him in the same quiet tones. But they cringed and bowed, and Hugh noticed that they avoided the look from Sir Henry's light-blue eyes.

That had been no surprise to Hugh. Sir Henry's name was an infamous one in all the towns and villages around the forest. Many people crossed themselves whenever he passed them, and few ever looked him in the face for more than a brief, fearful glance. He had seldom been known to raise his voice or to display a sign of anger, but he enjoyed cruelty, it was whispered, though some doubted that, for he always remained the same—calm, quiet, and completely emotionless.

Hugh rubbed his face. What Sir Henry would do to Jack and Roger was something he did not wish to think about. He went over to Geoffrey who was propped against a tree-trunk.

'How is it with you, Geoffrey?'

'Well enough, Hugh. They told you about Jack?'

'Yes.'

'You'd better find somewhere for us for the night.'

'Yes.'

Hugh turned away. For the moment there was nothing he could do about Jack. Sir Henry and his men would be clear of the forest by now, and in an hour they would be safe inside the walls of Goodrich Castle. Meanwhile there was plenty to do here, and he would have to give the orders and make the plans. Geoffrey would be of little help. He was a man of some learning, and extremely intelligent. With his great strength, his skill with the bow, and his brains, he could have made himself the undisputed leader of the outlaws long ago. But he was easy-going, lacking in any ambition, though he was a dangerous man when roused to anger. No sensible outlaw had provoked Geoffrey for a long time.

They spent an uncomfortable night under the trees, and during the following morning more of the outlaws drifted in from the forest, until there were over forty of them, Hugh estimated. They were ready enough to listen to him, and after they had collected what stores Sir Henry and his men had missed in the caves near the old camp, Hugh led them to the place he had discovered several years ago, a deep gorge with a wide stream running down on one side.

He started them working on the huts, and for the rest of the day he was giving orders, but still thinking of Jack. Already the glimmerings of a plan were forming in his head, and later that day he spoke to the outlaws. They shook their heads when he had finished. He cursed them angrily, and began again. There was silence this time, broken by Nick.

'I'll come with you, Hugh.'

'And I!' Will said.

The rest hesitated for a few seconds, and then they all jumped to their feet, shouting their agreement.

'Fetch the packs we took from the cave,' Hugh said. 'Nick, Will, you will come with me. Thomas, you will be in command of the rest. Now, listen!'

3
GOODRICH CASTLE

The great hall of Goodrich, on the first floor of the keep, was filled with all those who lived in the castle, for this was the time of the evening meal, the last of the day. The sun had not yet set, but as the windows were little more than slits in the thick walls, and the torches were still unlighted, much of the hall was in shadow.

On the dais at the far end tall candles had been placed on the table. Their soft light gleamed on the great salt-cellar in the centre, on the salvers and cups of silver, and on the two people who sat there under a velvet canopy, a scene that stood out in sharp relief against the near darkness of the rest of the hall. But those who were eating at the tables below seldom raised their eyes to look, and if they did so, they turned away hastily as if they had broken some strict rule. They talked in subdued tones and with an air of constraint.

Sir Henry Mortimer sat beneath the canopy in a high-backed chair, and with his wife by his side. Her clothes were rich and splendid, a surcote trimmed with fur, and with a mantle of blue velvet over her shoulders. Her hair was coiled in plaits over her ears, and held in place with golden clips. But despite her beautiful and costly appearance, her face was haggard and strained. She picked at her food, and her hands were trembling so much that when she reached for a cup of wine she knocked it over, and the contents ran slowly across the white cloth in a stream of deep red like blood.

Sir Henry glanced at her and then at the spilt wine. He said nothing, and there was no trace of anger, reproof, or sympathy, or indeed of any emotion at all on his long, pallid face. His light-blue eyes were as blank as those of a cat. But the Lady Mortimer winced as if she had been slashed by a whip across her thin shoulders.

He raised one long finger and two servants rushed forward

with napkins to mop up the wine, eyes averted and shoulders hunched like puppies expecting a beating.

Sir Henry went on calmly and silently with his meal. He was dressed with the same careful splendour as his wife, in a black velvet cotehardie with silver buttons, and scarlet mantle, a vivid streak of colour that dominated the whole scene under the candle-light, as indeed, he did, too, by the sheer force of his brooding silence and his cold, menacing personality. He sat upright with broad shoulders back, his cold eyes watching the servants or flickering slowly over the faces at the long tables. He saw the eyes turn away and his lips twitched slightly, as if in contempt.

He put down his knife, pushed away the silver plate, and stood up. A servant pulled away the chair, and Sir Henry, without bothering to see if his wife had finished her meal, stalked towards the door that led to the chamber, the private apartment of the lord of the castle. The Lady Mortimer flushed, dropped her knife and hurried after him, while the servants bowed and watched her with a very different expression, one of pity and affection, for she was a kindly woman and did much good, secretly and with stealth behind the back of her husband.

As the door of the chamber closed with a clang, a wave of relief seemed to rush over the hall. Voices rose, people laughed openly, and heads and shoulders came back as if those at the tables had felt a weight shift from their backs.

There were the usual visitors and travellers spending the night at the castle. Most of them were sitting at the table nearest the screens at the far end; a couple of pedlars, and two Franciscan friars in grey habits and cowls. The pedlars were young fellows, one with a freckled face and ears that stood out on each side of his head; the other was much taller, a powerfully built man with fair hair and a strong, determined face. Behind them on the floor were their packs, large and apparently crammed with the goods which they hoped to sell.

The Franciscans were both fat men, their habits stretched tightly around waist and chest, and like the pedlars', their faces, or what could be seen of them under the cowls, were burnt brown by the sun. But then, as everyone knew, pedlars and friars spent their days on the roads, travelling from town to town. These men, though, had little to say for themselves, and the castle servants who had been expecting to hear some

news of the world, had stopped asking questions, and had ignored them as surly, dull fellows.

The sun had gone down, and the torches fixed in brackets on the walls were being lighted. A man threw logs on the fire and kicked them into a cheerful blaze. The babble of voices rose higher, and at one table the laughter was almost continuous. A high-pitched and pleasant voice was telling some story, and then quoted a Latin tag. The fair-haired pedlar looked up sharply. For the first time he could now distinguish the faces of those at that table, and in the centre he saw a fat little man with a bald head.

'And what happened then, Ambrose?' someone asked.

Ambrose beamed happily at the upturned faces, and went on with his tale. As he finished a roar of laughter went up, and Ambrose, winecup raised, saw the pedlar staring at him. He hesitated, drained the cup, and rubbed his pointed, inquisitive nose. Someone refilled his beaker, and he swayed and hiccuped.

'Fresh air!' he said. 'I must have fresh air!' He stumbled and nearly fell, and they all laughed again as he walked unsteadily towards the screens.

The pedlar watched him go, and after a few seconds he stood up and followed. Ambrose was standing at the top of the steps leading down to the inner ward of the castle, and he turned and peered at the tall figure of the pedlar.

'Well, Master Hugh,' he said, and without a trace of drunkenness. 'What are you doing in the lion's den?'

'They have two of our men here,' Hugh said. 'Jack, and Roger Smith.' He slipped out his dagger, but Ambrose waved his hands.

'No need for that,' he said quickly. 'I have no love for Sir Henry Mortimer.'

'Who has? You will not give us away, then?'

'No, Master Hugh. But what can you do? You can't storm the castle.'

'I'm not going to try. But I must know where they are holding Jack and Roger.'

'I can find that for you from those men-at-arms at my table. But why not leave the castle while you have a whole skin, Master Hugh. I would not like to see Sir Henry's torturers at work on you.'

'I'll risk that.'

'So be it,' Ambrose said. He went back into the keep, and after a few minutes Hugh returned, too. Nick and the two 'friars' looked at him anxiously, but he shook his head to reassure them.

An hour later most of the torches had burnt out, and only a few people were still sitting at the tables. Many had gone to find a place elsewhere in the castle to sleep, and the rest were already snoring on the floor of the hall. Ambrose had told his last story, and to all appearance was hopelessly drunk. Hugh, pretending to sleep in his corner by the screens, watched him and smiled. At the camp he had seen the little doctor drink cup for cup with Jack, and it was Jack who had finished on the floor. Ambrose dropped his beaker with a clatter, belched, and lurched across the hall. He tripped and sprawled on the floor near Hugh.

'Magnum hoc vitio vinum est,' he said slowly. 'Pedes captat primum, luctator dolosus est.'

'And what does that mean, Ambrose?' the man-at-arms, who had been drinking with him, asked. He was drunk, too, and would be asleep in a few minutes, Hugh hoped.

'That is the great evil of wine,' Ambrose said. 'It first seizes the feet, and it is a cunning wrestler.'

They laughed again, the last laugh of the night, and drifted away, some outside the hall, and the others to straw pallets near the fire-place. Ambrose rolled over until his head was close to Hugh's.

'Your friends are in the castle jail,' he whispered.

'Where's that?'

'In the inner ward, against the curtain wall. To the left when you leave the keep. There is one sentry outside. There are more in the gatehouse, and two patrol the parapets at the top of the walls every hour.'

Hugh nodded, and turned over, pretending to sleep.

'The sentry has a key to the jail,' Ambrose muttered, and started to snore.

Hugh lay there for an hour and dozed. When he awoke the hall was in darkness, except for a red glow from the fire-place. The only sound was the gentle snoring of those asleep on the floor, and Hugh touched Nick's arm. The two 'friars' stood up, and followed Hugh and Nick as they tiptoed slowly through the screens.

At the end of the passage-way between the kitchens and the hall were the tall double doors leading to the inner keep. They were shut, and Hugh felt with his hands in the darkness for the huge iron handle. He touched a key, and turned it gently. It moved with a loud clank, and Nick hissed in panic. They waited, but though the key had made a noise that sounded like thunder in their nervous ears, they heard nothing from the hall. The hinges creaked as Hugh pulled the door towards them, and the outlaws slipped past him and out on to the steps. He took the key, pushed the door to, and turned the key before he hurled it away into the night.

'Wait!' he muttered.

They stood at the top of the steps, invisible, Hugh hoped, from the gatehouse, standing as they did in the shadow of the low wall that ran down one side of the steps. It was a dark night, and the moon had not yet risen. A strong wind had sprung up, and Hugh could hear the rustle of the trees on the other side of the curtain wall.

His eyes were more accustomed to the darkness now, and he could distinguish the outlines of the castle. Below was the wide open space of the inner ward separated by a narrow ditch from the mound on which stood the keep. Opposite was the gatehouse with its two towers, and all around were the tall walls of the curtain, with projecting towers at regular intervals, their outlines black against the dark grey of the sky. To the left was a line of lean-to buildings, and there, according to Ambrose, was the castle jail.

There would be sentries on the wall, too, he had said, but if they saw anyone coming out of the keep they would not raise an alarm. It was danger from outside they would be guarding against, though there was peace in the country under the firm rule of King Edward, and sentries were posted only as a gesture in most castles. Not even Sir Henry Mortimer would be expecting an attack on his castle in the middle of a summer's night, and he would not be afraid of the outlaws. To storm such a castle as Goodrich would need hundreds of men, scaling-ladders, moveable towers, and all the elaborate machinery of a full-scale siege.

'Keep behind me,' Hugh said, and walked down the steps, over the wooden bridge that spanned the ditch, and there he stopped. This was the danger spot, the open stretch of the bailey between the ditch and the jail.

'Wait here! Run over when I whistle!'

He walked forward leisurely, though his heart was pounding, and his fists were clenched. But he hoped that the sentry would not be startled by the approach of one man. If he saw four coming towards him he would naturally be suspicious.

'Who's that?' a voice asked.

Hugh saw the figure standing in the shadow of the buildings, and the dull gleam of his helmet. He went on steadily at the same deliberate pace.

'It's Thomas Hood, a pedlar,' he said. 'I've been sick.'

'Too much wine,' the sentry said. 'You're lucky. I haven't had a perishing drop since midday.'

'You can finish mine,' Hugh said, and held out a flask.

The sentry seized it and raised it to his lips. As he put his head back to drink, Hugh's fingers closed on his throat, fingers and wrists strengthened by years of holding and drawing a long-bow. Without a sound the man's knees began to buckle, and Hugh lowered him gently to the ground. He turned his head and whistled. Three dark figures flitted across the bailey. Hugh was bending over the sentry and held up a key.

'Tie his hands and gag him,' he muttered.

Nick opened one of the large packs and brought out short lengths of cord and a rag which he stuffed into the sentry's mouth. Hugh turned the lock in the door of the jail, and peered into the stuffy darkness. He heard a rustle of someone moving on straw, and the clink of a chain.

'Who's there?' a hoarse voice asked.

'Hugh. Is that you, Jack?'

'Hugh! How . . .'

'Quiet! Are you chained to the wall?'

'Yes, so's Roger. That sentry has the key. In his pouch.'

'Nick! Find that key! Quick!'

Nick yelped and turned the sentry over, while Hugh felt in the darkness for the lock that held the chain.

'Here you are, Hugh!' Nick pressed a key into his hand.

'Right, Jack! Roger, hold out the lock!'

'How are you going to get us out of this hell hole?' Jack asked. 'We can't walk through the gatehouse, boy?'

'You'll see,' Hugh said. 'Come on!'

Jack paused outside and bent over the sentry. He spat and kicked the man viciously in the ribs.

'Give me your dagger, boy,' he said.

'Leave him, you fool! Come on!'

'He kicked out one of my best teeth today. Just a taste of what Sir Henry would do in the morning,' Jack said. His foot thudded into the man's ribs again, and Hugh dragged him away impatiently.

'Up the steps to the parapet!' he said. 'Hurry, or you won't have any teeth left if Sir Henry catches us!'

They all tore up the narrow stone steps to the top of the curtain wall, and Hugh put his fingers to his mouth and whistled shrilly.

'Ropes!' he said. 'Out with them!'

The two outlaws dressed as friars ripped off their long habits and began to unwind the long ropes that were coiled around their waists and chests, and which had made them appear so portly. Nick was pulling out another rope from one of the packs.

'The loops here!' Hugh said. They fixed them around two merlons, the raised stone between the embrasures of the parapet, and dropped the ropes over the wall.

'Jack and Roger, go first!'

'What about the other side of the ditch?' Roger asked.

'Thomas and the rest will be there. They'll throw you ropes and pull you up. Hurry, man, hurry!'

Hugh whistled again, and leant over the wall, staring into the night. He grunted as he heard an answering whistle, and saw a line of dark figures run out of the trees towards the ditch below.

Jack and Roger were in the ditch now, and ropes were being dropped down to them by the outlaws.

'You two next!' Hugh said to the 'friars'. 'Nick, you and I last!'

A shout came from the right, and there was the sound of feet running along the parapet. Hugh spun round. He saw a man rushing along the wall towards them, vanishing inside one of the towers, and then bursting through the open door about twenty paces away. He waved his sword as he saw Hugh and Nick, and shouted.

From the ditch came the twang of bows, and Hugh could hear the whistle of the shafts. Two whizzed over the top of the parapet and vanished into the darkness. The sentry yelled and staggered. As he overbalanced and plunged down into the bailey, he screeched with pain and terror.

'Nick!' Hugh shouted. 'You next!'

He watched Nick lower himself over the wall, and then did the same, gripping the thick rope with hands and feet. As he began to slide down, bumping against the stonework, shouts came from the direction of the keep, and a trumpet sounded shrilly from the gatehouse. Hugh smiled as he let himself drop. They would have to break open the doors of the keep. The rope was burning the palms of his hands, and then his feet hit the side of the sloping ditch, and he let go. He rolled and bumped to the bottom with a thud, and as he stood up a voice yelled at him from above, and he saw the end of a rope. He grasped it with both hands, and struggled up the steep bank to finish on the ground at the top, panting from his exertions.

Someone hauled him to his feet, and Jack was shouting hoarsely.

'Thomas!' Hugh yelled. 'Thomas! Where are the horses?'

'By the trees, Hugh! Loose! Loose!'

A volley of shafts hissed away and up into the dark sky, and then the outlaws turned and raced for the shelter of the trees and the horses that Hugh had ordered Thomas to bring with him. There were not enough for all of them, and some of the horses carried two riders, as they galloped away into the forest.

Hugh heard the trumpets still pealing from the castle. He laughed and shook his reins, and bent low in the saddle as a branch scraped his shoulders. They would never be caught now, and he shouted with delight.

4

SIR HENRY MORTIMER

At dawn the next morning Hugh collected all the outlaws. After the astonishing success of the rescue of Jack and Roger from Goodrich Castle they listened to Hugh in a respectful silence.

'Sir Henry will be after us again,' he said.

'If he can find us here,' Nick pointed out.

'He'll bring his hounds with him,' Hugh said. 'Today or tomorrow.'

The outlaws looked at one another uneasily, and one man suggested that they should leave the forest altogether and take to the mountains. But Hugh shook his head.

'We can hold him off here,' he said. 'If we post sentries on each side of the gorge we shall have plenty of time. I want four men; the rest of you will be shown your positions when the alarm is given, and until then get on with the huts.'

The gorge, as he had known, was an ideal place for defence. High walls of rock rose on either side; the stream widened out into a deep pool in the centre, and there was ample room for the huts and the vegetable plots and fields that Hugh had planned beside the pool and the cliff on that side. The entrances to the gorge at both ends were narrow and could be held by skilled bowmen with ease, so long as they were given time to take up their positions. He posted two sentries in the trees at each entrance, and then showed the others where they were to go when the warning-signal was given. After that he set them to work building, each man with his bow and a full quiver on the ground by his side.

That Sir Henry would search the forest for them with a cold and ruthless fury was a certainty, and his hounds would lead him to the gorge without much doubt. Hugh could well imagine Sir Henry's mood, his feeling of bitter shame at that impudent rescue from the depths of his castle, a story that could make him the laughing-stock of the countryside, for he had no friends, and even some of the other barons in the area might chuckle when they heard what had happened. Perhaps, Hugh thought, it might have been as well for that sentry if Jack had cut his throat. Sir Henry would not deal very gently with him. But Hugh had little sympathy to spare for men who served Sir Henry. Roger had one rib broken, and Jack had been knocked about badly by the men-at-arms as they took him back to the castle after the raid on the old camp.

But there was no alarm that day, and the outlaws spent the night under what shelters they had already built. One party had brought in some venison, and the older men and the children had caught fish in the pool, so that they were not short of food. The next morning was fine and hot, and Hugh sat by the pool, his bow by his side, and waited, while around him the outlaws went on with their work at the new huts. The gorge became hot and oppressive as the sun rose overhead, and Hugh closed his eyes and dozed.

He awoke as someone shook his arm. It was Nick, his freckled face alight with excitement.

'Hounds, Hugh! The baying of hounds!'

Hugh stood up slowly and stretched his long arms. It was a relief after the long wait to know that the matter was going to be settled at last. He laughed at Nick's anxious face, and picked up his bow.

'Tell the men to take up their positions,' he said.

He went round the posts, speaking to each man, and telling them to hold their fire until the last possible moment, though there was little fear of that. They were all skilled bowmen, and they would be fighting in their element, the forest.

Only then did he go to his own post at the northern end of the ravine, the most open and vulnerable of the two approaches. He stood on the highest point of a low ridge. In front the ground was covered with an outcrop of rocks, and he was well hidden by tall grass. He pulled out a dozen shafts from his quiver, and stuck them head down into the ground so that he could snatch them up quickly. Half of them were hunting shafts, but the rest had war-heads with a bodkin-shaped tip capable of penetrating armour.

From what he had seen at Goodrich, Sir Henry's men would be wearing helmets and brigandines; these were thick leather coats on which plates of steel were sewn. Sir Henry and his squires, and he had three, so Hugh knew, would almost certainly be in mail—and with the many steel plates that were being added now to a knight's equipment, covering the arms and legs. There would probably be some bowmen, too, but the total force would be small.

Hugh lifted his head. Hounds were baying in the distance. He had heard hounds many times before, but it was an uneasy sensation to know that he was the quarry this time. A horn sounded, and Hugh stood up, shaft on the string, tense and alert. The hounds must be closer than he had thought, and they were coming to this end of the ravine, as he had guessed.

He glanced down at the shaft, a broadhead, for the first to show would be the horsemen, and he would aim at the horses. The hounds would be no danger, probably. They were trained to go for deer and wild boar, not men.

He stood amidst the bracken with the hot sun on his face, tall and stolid, with the great bow in his hands. But his fingers were trembling slightly. This was his responsibility. It was he who had persuaded the outlaws to stay and fight it out. If he was wrong, he had condemned them all to a fearful death. Sir Henry's vengeance would be merciless, a story that would be retailed around the countryside with low whispers and staring eyes.

Two hounds sprang into sight, and then the whole pack burst out of the trees and surged down the narrow track between the rocks. The horn sounded again, quite close, and four horsemen trotted out into the open, and the sun flashed and glittered on their armour.

In the lead was Sir Henry. There was no mistaking him in his mail and plate, and the close-fitting black jupon over his mail, embroidered with his crest of a lion's head. He was wearing a bascinet on his head, the new type of helmet with a face piece that could be moved up and down on hinges. It was raised now, and the knight was leaning forward in his saddle, urging on the hounds. By his side was a huntsman, and then came two young squires, both in mail and plate and, like Sir Henry, carrying shields painted with their coats of arms.

Up came Hugh's bow, his left hand aiming at Sir Henry's

horse, his right hand coming back to his ear until the great bow was at full stretch. The string twanged and the thin, deadly shaft whistled over the rocks and plunged remorselessly into the chest of the horse. The wretched animal reared up under the sudden shock and the burning pain of his wound. Sir Henry shouted, and wrestled to control his maddened horse. Hugh was drawing again with the speed and precision of the master bowman, and another shaft hit the horse. It galloped madly to one side. An overhanging branch swept Sir Henry from his saddle, and even at that distance Hugh heard the clang of his armour as he hit the ground with a shattering crash.

The other concealed bowmen were loosing now, loosing at ease and with the priceless advantage of complete surprise. The huntsman was down, his horse riddled with shafts, and with one through his leg. One of the squires had been thrown, and the other had been carried back into the trees by his horse.

Hugh smiled. The tension had gone now. His fingers were firm and steady as he nocked his third shaft. Sir Henry was lying still, stunned probably by his fall. Four mounted men-at-arms galloped into the open. A dozen shafts leapt at them. One horse fell immediately. The others swerved away as they were hit and vanished into the trees again.

Hugh had not loosed. He stood there waiting. The bowmen and any others on foot that Sir Henry could have mustered would come next. Well, the outlaws were ready for them. As for the hounds, they had disappeared down the track, and they were probably playing with the children in the gorge by this time. They had done their work, and had brought Sir Henry into as deadly an ambush as any soldier could have wished for.

A line of bowmen ran, a squire on foot waving them forward. They halted and up came their bows. But they were too slow. A volley of shafts swooped down upon them with a fearful accuracy, and then another, the shafts leaving the bows before the first flight had landed. Hugh still waited. He saw a bowman on the right of the line still standing, and slowly and carefully Hugh moved his left fist to the right, and then he loosed. Calmly he watched the shaft as it hurtled down. He heard the screech as the bowman crumpled to the ground, clutching with both hands at the feathers of the shaft that had smashed through the plates of his brigandine.

Those of the bowmen who had not been hit had scurried back into the safety of the trees, leaving nearly a dozen on the ground, some of them with two arrows driven through them. They should all have been down, Hugh thought angrily. The outlaws needed practice, and he would see that they got it in the next few weeks.

A trumpet blew in the forest. The two heavily armed squires ran out on foot, waving on the bowmen and a ragged line of men with spears. Hugh drew and loosed in a flash, and was nocking once more without bothering to see whether his shaft had hit or not. As he came up to the aim again he saw the air filled with a steady rain of arrows from the hidden outlaws, flying from the bushes and rocks towards the mob ahead, for that was what it had become in a matter of a couple of minutes. The spearmen—villeins pressed unwillingly into service, Hugh guessed, and without the protection of brigandines—had turned and fled, leaving half a dozen bodies behind. The bowmen had loosed about a dozen shafts, almost blindly, for

the outlaws were scattered, and kept moving to different positions as Hugh had taught them the evening before.

Then they were all gone, either dead on the ground, or back once more in the trees, and Hugh knew that they would not come out again. The squires, crouching behind their shields, were unhurt. They had stopped, dismayed to find that they were alone, and every outlaw loosed at them. The shafts rained down upon them; one dropped his shield, his arm pierced by an arrow. As he crawled away, three more shafts swooped down and pinned him to the ground. The other turned and ran. Grimly Hugh drew and aimed with care, his mouth set remorselessly. He had heard unpleasant tales of Sir Henry's squires. Like master, like man, he thought as he loosed. No good man would have stayed long in the service of such a knight. The squire threw his arms up and staggered forward like a drunken man as Hugh's shaft caught him high on the shoulder, and then a dozen shafts seemed to fall on him at once, and he fell flat on his face, perfectly still, and even at that distance Hugh could see the feathers sticking up from his back and legs.

There was silence, and a long pause, but no one appeared from the trees.

'Wait!' Hugh yelled. 'Wait! Keep your positions!'

This might be a trap to lure the outlaws into the open, but Sir Henry was still lying by a rock; his squires were dead, and there was no one to lead a fresh attack. The hounds came flooding back from the gorge and disappeared into the trees, one or two pausing to sniff at the dead huntsman, and then they had all gone, and the sun shone down peacefully, and the outlaws stood patiently, and waited. They had learned to obey Hugh now. He was always right, and they had won a startling victory. It would be a long time before Sir Henry or anyone else for that matter would venture into the forest again to attack them.

'Forward!' Hugh shouted. 'Nick! Take six men into the trees as sentries. Warn us if they come again.'

The outlaws swarmed down the slope, and started to strip the bodies of everything of value, rifling pouches, ripping off the armour from the squires—a valuable piece of loot that—and picking up fallen shafts which had taken many patient hours to shape and smooth.

Hugh ran forward and bent over Sir Henry Mortimer. Jack joined him, and pulled up the front of the bascinet.

'Still alive,' he said.

Sir Henry looked up at them with a puzzled expression for a few seconds, and then his face went blank. He sat up, and then slowly got to his feet, leaning back against a tree.

Jack tugged out his dagger, and Sir Henry watched him as he looked down at the blade and at the knight.

'No!' Hugh said sharply.

'Now, why not, Hugh?'

'Not in cold blood like this, Jack.'

Jack spat and growled. Sir Henry was staring at Hugh, though whether it was with curiosity or gratitude for saving his life, it would have been impossible to say.

'You'll get no thanks from him,' Jack said in disgust.

'I don't want any.' Hugh turned to Sir Henry, who was still examining him.

'I will know you again,' the knight said quietly.

'And I you, my lord.'

Some emotion flickered in the light-blue eyes. 'Were you the man who freed my prisoners?' he asked.

'Yes, my lord.'

'It was well planned. I could make good use of you.'

Hugh started with surprise, and Sir Henry smiled coldly.

'Why not?' he asked. 'Or do you think that would be a trap, so that I could hang you at my leisure?'

Hugh shook his head. 'No, my lord. I believe you. But I would take service with any other lord in England before I would accept your offer.'

'Then I will certainly hang you when I can,' Sir Henry said.

He turned, and walked away slowly into the forest, while Hugh rubbed his chin.

'The odd thing is that I believed him,' he said to Jack.

'That he'd hang you? You can believe that, boy.'

'No, Jack. That he really wanted me to enter his service, and that it was not a trap to catch me.'

'The only odd thing, you young fool, is that you didn't let me cut his perishing throat.' Jack spat with unusual force. 'Come on, before those thieves down there pinch my share of the loot. Those squires should have something in their pouches.'

5

WATKYN THE BOWYER

Hugh lay at full length in the long grass, perfectly still, his eyes on the stream below, listening and waiting with the fierce, patient persistence of the trained hunter. A few feet away was Nick, his head down as he watched a group of ants running busily to and fro amidst the grass.

'Hist!' Nick looked up quickly, and his ears twitched. Two roe-deer had trotted quietly up to the stream, just as Hugh had expected. He knew this particular spot, where there was water and rich grass. Years ago as a boy he had been taught that the animals of the forest did not wander about aimlessly. When they moved, they did so with a purpose, and often at definite times of the day. Soon after dawn like this particular moment, or at dusk, were the best times for hunting deer, and Hugh preferred dawn.

Two shafts lay by his side. However careful a bowman might be, a shaft rustled as it was drawn from a quiver, and even the slightest sound might scare off the deer. These were hunting shafts with a broad head, for the smooth war-heads would have gone clean through a deer, driven by the terrific velocity of a long-bow. But Hugh was carrying a shorter one that morning.

To loose his great bow he must stand to his full height, and the deer would be off before he had brought his hand back to his ear. This shorter bow he could draw to his mouth, and so aim along the line of the shaft for greater accuracy. He could draw while kneeling, too, and deadly accuracy to an inch was what he needed now. No forester relished a long and difficult chase through the forest after a wounded deer.

He watched the deer and estimated the range, for once he started to draw, he must loose immediately. About thirty paces, he reckoned. Anything much longer than that would be a difficult shot in the forest, where the lower branches of the trees would deflect the shaft. At a hundred paces the arrow rose quite twenty feet in the air, so that a bowman seldom aimed directly at his mark, and only years of practice and experience helped him to judge how much to allow for the fall of his shaft.

There was no such problem here. The flight would be quite flat, and Hugh could take an aim for the heart of the deer. There was a very slight breeze from right to left, not strong enough to push his arrow off the line at thirty paces.

The deer had stopped now after a cautious inspection of the ground around them, and down went their heads as they started to nibble at the grass. Just below the shoulder was Hugh's mark, where the shaft would smash through the great arteries of the heart, causing instant death. A fraction or so above or below, and the deer might run for a mile before dropping, and even a born forester such as Hugh would need all his lore to follow the trail. And that would be a bungled shot, and Hugh with his fierce persistence and pride in his craft detested slipshod work.

Slowly and with infinite care he took a shaft and nocked it. An inch or so at a time he drew up his long legs until he was kneeling, and then he began to draw. On his right Nick was doing the same, but he would not loose until Hugh did. Nobody in the outlaws' camp ever did much now before Hugh had given his approval.

Hugh squinted along the slim shaft. His strong fingers relaxed their grip on the string, and it sprang forward. The shaft swooped across the grass, and out of the corner of his eye

Hugh saw the grey, flickering blur of the feathers on Nick's arrow.

Hugh watched his own shaft with the deep satisfaction of a clean, smooth loose as it flew straight and true, driving into the deer at the exact spot for which he had aimed. Both deer went down on their knees, struggling to stand again, and then they rolled over and lay still.

'He! He!' Nick yelled in the age-old cry of the bowman greeting a clean hit. He jumped to his feet, waved his bow in the air, and rushed through the long grass, yelping with delight.

Hugh smiled and walked after him. He would have liked to shout and run, too, but he was the leader of the outlaws. He ruled by the force of his personality and his intelligence, and he could not unbend, he felt, or display the immature excitement of a young man. But he was a young man still, for all that.

They looked down at the deer, and nodded to each other, the solid sense of achievement after a long and patient wait, and then the clean, accurate kill. Then with a sigh they started the labour of the long haul back to the gorge.

As they approached the northern end of the ravine, Hugh stopped and whistled. An answering whistle came from the trees ahead, and a small boy slid down the trunk of one, and waved his hand.

'Was that all right, Hugh?' he asked, and there was a distinct note of anxiety in his voice.

'Did you hear us before I whistled, Tom?'

'Yes, Hugh. But only a rustle in the grass. I wasn't certain it was you and Nick.'

'Good! You did well, Tom.' Hugh smiled, the charming and friendly smile that Ambrose had noticed, and the boy flushed with pleasure before he climbed back to his perch. He would have been thrashed if he had fallen asleep or failed to give warning of the approach of a stranger, but he knew with equal certainty that he would be praised by Hugh if he did his work well.

It was two years since Sir Henry Mortimer had made his unsuccessful attack on the gorge, and nobody else had made a similar attempt. In that time Hugh had transformed the place. Long rows of well-built huts stood in orderly lines, and the whole camp was clean and neat. Around each hut was a small vegetable plot, and farther down the gorge were crops of barley and wheat. But the main income of the outlaws came from their horses which they sold in all the towns and villages around the forest.

Though most people with whom they dealt knew who and what they were, they were safe enough. They never robbed travellers on the roads, and so they were left alone. But that was not the only reason for their immunity. They were nearly a hundred strong now, well-disciplined fine bowmen, and living in the depths of a vast forest. No sensible man would venture to disturb such a hornets nest. Only once, a year ago, the steward of a manor had hoped for a reward if he delivered an outlaw to the sheriff of Skenfrith, and he had ordered two frightened villeins to lock the man up. They had freed him during the night, and the next morning the steward had stormed angrily out of his house. A dozen cloth-yard shafts hissed out from the trees on the other side of the road, and the man was pinned against his own door.

That was warning enough, and the news had spread. The name of Hugh Fletcher, the leader of this formidable band, was well known; there was not a man for miles around who would have laid a hand on him or any of his friends.

As for Sir Henry, he had not been seen at Goodrich during those two years. He was serving in Normandy with the King's troops there, for it was well known that he was heavily in debt, and hoped to pick up some rich ransoms to clear himself.

Hugh went to the largest hut, which he shared with Jack and Geoffrey. They were sitting outside on stools, intent on the delicate task of glueing feathers to their shafts, and Hugh lay on the grass and watched them. Geoffrey picked up a piece of thread and wound it round a feather; once the glue had set he would cut away the thread and trim the feathers. He glanced up at the sky. Some white clouds were drifting overhead, and he nodded. A cloudy day, so the old bowmen said, was essential for fletching, the art of making arrow shafts, though Hugh could not for the life of him understand why that should be so. But it was one of the ancient rules of their craft, and they observed it whenever they could.

Not far away a line of boys was drawn up facing a straw butt, and Jack strolled over to them. Each boy held a bow cut to match his height, and this was the time for their morning lesson.

'Practice for standing!' Jack rasped in his hoarse voice. 'Feet apart, chest to the right! Head to the left!'

They shuffled into position, but were not fast enough for Jack.

'Quicker than that, you perishing snails!' he shouted. They tried again, and then for a third time, until he was satisfied. 'Chests out! Bellies in!' He prodded a boy with the end of a long cane he was carrying. 'In, Walter! Now, ready for it! STAND!'

Up went a dozen arms, each stretched out rigidly. But they were not to Jack's satisfaction.

'Straighter! And keep yer perishing eyes on the mark!'

Jack nodded, and strolled up and down behind the boys, whistling softly. Five long minutes passed. One small arm began to droop. THWACK! The cane swished down on the back of the boy's legs. He yelped like a puppy, and up came his arm again.

Hugh grinned. Years ago he had been taught like that until his left arm had ached like fire, and his legs were covered with

weals from a cane. But drawing a long-bow was an exhausting exercise; it was not only a matter of sheer strength; skill and practice were essential, too, but the muscles of arm and wrist and fingers had to be hardened to stand the tremendous strain, so that a bowman could pull back the immensely thick limbs of the bow to their full extent again and again, and throughout a battle, if need be.

Hugh strolled down to a group of men who were cutting up the deer that he and Nick had killed that morning. Hugh wanted some of the sinews for fresh binding on the grips of his bows. That would be a tedious task, scraping the sinews, beating them with a mallet, softening them in water, more scraping, and then hanging them up to dry until they turned to a deep amber colour. There were several such bundles hanging in the hut, but every bowman liked to have a reserve supply.

One man was hacking off a large piece of venison, and making an untidy job of it. Hugh frowned. He disliked the fellow, who called himself Sim, and who had arrived in the gorge the day before, asking for shelter. He had said he was a runaway villein who had fled to escape a beating, but Hugh did not believe him. The man was a townsman, and probably a thief, if not a murderer into the bargain. He carried a dagger, and often fingered it nervously. He would not stay in the gorge long, Hugh decided. The small group of outlaws who sat with Hugh and Geoffrey to discuss the affairs of the camp examined each new recruit, and they would certainly reject Sim. He was no bowman, and no forester, either.

'That's my deer, Sim,' Hugh said quietly. 'You can take what you want when we've finished with it.'

Sim looked up and smirked with what he hoped was an ingratiating smile. He carried his head on one side, and he walked with an ungainly shuffle. Unlike the men around him, with faces burnt a dark brown by sun and wind, he was pallid, and he sniffed continuously as if he had a permanent cold.

'Share and share alike, Master Fletcher,' he said. 'That's the rule, isn't it?'

'No, it's not. You take your share of the work, though, and I haven't seen you do any of that yet.'

Sim sniffed. 'Give me a chance, Master Fletcher.'

'Then you can start now. Drop that venison, and chop that wood over there.'

Sim flushed, and his eyes blazed with fury. 'Now, see here, Master Fletcher, I don't take orders from any man.'

The other outlaws stared at him in astonishment. They were a tough, determined crowd of men, but not one of them would have dared to speak to Hugh like that. They would not have done so, in any case, for they respected and liked him. But Sim took no notice of the sly grins on their faces as they waited for Hugh to deal with him. He stood up and glared at Hugh, and his hand went to his dagger.

Hugh's long arm shot out like a shaft from his bow. His clenched fist caught Sim full on his nose, and he went flat on his back. He rolled over, one hand to his aching nose, and the other holding the dagger. Hugh put his foot on his wrist, and Sim yelled. The dagger fell away, and Hugh hauled him to his feet.

'Go and chop wood,' he said, and flung him away.

Slim shuffled away, head to one side, and one hand still pressed to his nose.

'Have a care, Hugh,' one of the men said. 'Sim's a dagger man. In your back.'

Hugh returned to the hut. The long winter was not far away, he thought, and he frowned. He detested the winter, with the bare dripping trees of the forest, the mists, the rain, and the cold winds that howled through the gorge. There was little comfort inside the huts, however well-built they were. The fire kept them warm, but the smoke made their eyes run, and everything was damp. The nights were long, and the flickering rushlights gave nothing more than a faint glow; there was little you could do once the sun went down but huddle under blankets and skins, and wait for the dawn.

Geoffrey was lying on the grass, his fletching done. He was an immense figure, lying there, the tallest and strongest man in the camp. Probably the cleverest, too, Hugh thought irritably. He had a great affection for Geoffrey, but he wished he would make more use of his advantages of body and brain. He sighed, and took down his long-bow from a rack on the wall of the hut. He was not happy about it. There was a tendency to kick at the moment of loosing, which jarred his left hand, and upset the aim. He would consult Jack, he decided. All the outlaws went to Jack with their problems about bows, for he was a master bowman. When he drew his great bow his stocky, muscular body became a picture of grace; he could nock, draw, and loose with a smooth precision, speed and accuracy that was a delight to watch, and the envy of any bowman who knew how difficult was the art of using a long-bow.

The boys were still in a line, and Jack was teaching them how to nock the shaft to the string.

'First finger on the string,' he growled. 'Second and third below. Get the string in the crease of your finger joints. Don't touch the perishing shaft, Hal!' The cane swished down. Hal shut his mouth, and screwed up his face with the pain. It was a point of honour among the boys that they tried not to yelp when Jack beat them.

'Your fingers are there to pull the string,' Jack said. 'Not to hold the shaft. It'll stay on the string without your stupid fingers holding it. What do you think the perishing string is for?'

He went down the line inspecting each boy's hand.

'Now we'll try drawing,' he said. 'Keep your eyes on the clout, Edward.' Another whistle from the cane. Little Edward shut his eyes for a moment, and then opened them to stare fiercely at the white rag that acted as an aiming mark.

'When I shout DRAW,' Jack said, 'bring up your bows and start drawing. Push with the left hand, pull with the right, and pull with your arms and legs and shoulders and backs. Lay your perishing bodies into the bow!' He paused. 'DRAW!'

The bows came up steadily, and began to bend in graceful arcs.

'If anyone drops his shaft I'll whack all the dust out of his hose! Keep your thumbs off the heel of the shaft. That's what makes it drop.'

One shaft did drop. The small culprit looked down fearfully.

'Pick it up, Piers!'

Piers bent down. The cane whistled down on his tightly stretched hose, and he straightened himself with a jerk, his eyes filled with tears.

'Nock and draw again, Piers,' Jack said.

Piers tried to do as he was told, but his fingers were shaking, and the shaft fell for the second time. He braced himself for the lash of the cane, his eyes shut.

'Now, boy,' Jack said, and his hoarse voice was curiously gentle, 'try again. You can do it.'

Piers grinned, and this time he drew the string back, his small body stiff and erect. Hugh smiled. Jack was an odd mixture of ruthless toughness and unexpected kindness.

Jack ended the lesson, and strolled up to where Hugh was sitting.

'This bow of mine,' Hugh said, 'do you . . .'

'Whip ended,' Jack said. 'The wood wasn't properly seasoned. A good bowyer leaves a piece of wood for five years at least before he uses it.'

Hugh looked unhappily at his great bow. There were some competent bowyers among the outlaws, but he wanted the best this time, a bow made by a master craftsman.

'Go to old Watkyn at Fingle Cross,' Jack said. 'He'll want a good price, though.'

Hugh left the gorge after dawn the next morning, bound for Fingle Cross, which was a village to the west of the forest. He went on foot, for he felt restless, and the long walk would suit his mood better than riding. This restlessness was something he could not explain, though once he had realized with a shock of discomfort that he was evading the answer, and he tried not to think about it again. But he had suddenly discovered that he was tired of his life in the forest, and that he wanted a life that would be completely different.

Fingle Cross was a large manor, part of the lands of the Bishop of Gloucester, and was administered for him by a bailiff and a reeve who lived in the largest houses. As it was on the main road to the west, there was a good inn, and Watkyn's workshop, so Jack had said, was not far from there.

The innkeeper was standing outside in the road when Hugh came up the long street of huts. He looked sharply at Hugh, for he had recognized him, and greeted him respectfully.

'Watkyn the Bowyer, Master Fletcher,' he said, 'you will find him in his shed. There!' and he pointed. 'He will make you a fine bow.'

Behind the hut that Hugh had been shown was a long, lean-to shed, and he could hear the rasp of a saw. He pushed open the door, a well-made one, he noticed with approval, and found himself in a room filled with the pleasant scent of freshly-sawn wood. A white-haired man was bending over a bench at the far end, and he turned to look at his visitor.

'Are you Watkyn the Bowyer?'

'I am, young sir.' Watkyn was an old man, his face a network of fine wrinkles, a placid kindly face, with a pair of shrewd eyes that were examining Hugh with great interest.

'Jack Cherryman sent me,' Hugh said. 'He said you would make me a good bow.'

'Jack!' The old face broke into a hundred thin lines of pleasure. 'And you, I think, are Master Hugh Fletcher. But you have a bow already.'

'It kicks,' Hugh said.

Watkyn took the bow. His long fingers stroked the wood, and he peered at the grain before he pulled the string back slowly several times.

'Whip ended,' he said sadly. 'Unseasoned wood.' He put the bow down carefully, but with a gesture that showed he had no further interest in such a poor piece of craftsmanship. 'I can make you a better bow than that, Master Fletcher.'

'Can I choose my own stave?'

Watkyn pointed to a rack filled with yew staves. 'They are all seasoned pieces, not a stave under seven years.'

He watched Hugh turn over the long staves, and smiled. All young bowmen insisted on picking out their own staves, but they seldom chose the best one.

'This one,' Hugh said decisively.

Watkyn's smile disappeared, and he eyed Hugh with an added respect. The stave was straight grained and completely free of knots, and it was one that he had been keeping for the day when he would produce one of his masterpieces.

'That is my best stave,' he said. 'This will be an expensive bow, Master Fletcher.'

'Jack said you would not cheat me. I want a fine bow, Watkyn. How much?'

'Three nobles. I am a master bowyer.'

It was a high price, but Hugh did not hesitate. He had taken a liking to old Watkyn, and he could well afford the money, for he had a considerable amount hidden away in the forest.

He took the stick that Watkyn gave him and held it out at the full stretch of his left arm while the bowyer measured the distance between his fingers and the point of his jaw, and then back to his ear, for that would be the extent of his draw.

Hugh started back immediately for the gorge. He was excited at the prospect of using his new bow, for it would almost certainly be the finest he had ever owned. His mind, too, was filled with plans for the winter, the storing of salted meat, the repair of the worst huts, and the collection of firewood. But absorbed as he was, his forester's instincts were still aware of what was going on around him. He heard a rustle in the trees to his right, and then the snap of dry wood underfoot. He stopped and turned as two men leapt out from behind a tree and barred the track he was following.

He recognized them immediately. One was Sim, and the other was a man called Owen, who had come to the gorge with Sim. Jack had accused him of trying to steal a jerkin, and had knocked him down. Both men had daggers in their hands, thumb over the hilt, point upwards, and they ran towards Hugh in silence, murder in every line of their wolfish faces.

Hugh jumped back, and his hand went to his belt. But he had left his sword in the gorge. His bow was useless at this range. He turned to run, and his foot caught in a tree root. He stumbled, put out his arm and saved himself from falling by leaning against a tree. He moved again, and this time, for he dared not take his eyes from the two men, he tripped once more, and went flat on his back. He heard Sim's high-pitched yelp, and he knew that he was helpless, trapped by two men who would cut his throat without the slightest compunction.

6

THE NEW BOW

Hugh rolled over in the undergrowth, fumbling with one hand for his dagger, expecting at every moment to feel the searing pain of Sim's or Owen's knife in his side. Something hissed over him. Owen screamed suddenly and horribly. Hugh was up on his knees to see Sim standing still, mouth open in horror. Owen was propped against a tree-trunk, eyes turned up, his fingers scrabbling at the feathers of an arrow that had suddenly appeared in the centre of his chest. Sim flung himself on the ground with a yell and another shaft whistled over his head. Hugh scrambled to his feet and leapt at Sim, battering his face with his clenched fists.

'He! He!' a voice shouted, and Nick came bounding through the trees, waving his bow. 'Don't kill him, Hugh,' he said, bending over Sim. 'Tie his hands with this.' He twisted a bow-string around Sim's wrists, and tightened the knot with a vicious jerk that made the fellow howl.

'You'll get worse than that in the gorge,' Nick said. He kicked Sim in the ribs, 'Get up! Walk!'

'What about Owen?' Hugh asked.

'Dead,' Nick said, grinning with delight. 'A sweet roving shaft, Hugh. I wish Jack could have seen it.'

'But how did you come here?'

'I saw this pair leave the gorge. They don't hunt, so I followed them.'

'It was lucky you did,' Hugh said. He smiled at Nick. 'Thank you, Nick.'

Nick flushed and stammered, still grinning with pleasure at his good shot and his delight in having done something for Hugh.

A curious crowd collected around them when they reached the gorge, and Nick began to explain what had happened. But Hugh cut him short.

'Wait, Nick. Let the court decide.'

Hugh had set up a court of the older men to judge disputes and to deal with offenders against the rules he had laid down. Geoffrey, by common consent the most learned man in the camp, acted as the judge, and asked most of the questions. It was rough justice, but fair, and no outlaw had as yet disputed the verdicts of the court.

Hugh acted as the chief witness, and then Nick added his version. Jack took a professional interest in the shot that had killed Owen, and then nodded appreciatively, which made Nick grin even more widely. Sim, hands still tied behind his back, shuffled his feet and listened with a scowl to everything that was said, his eyes shifting uneasily from one face to another.

'Well, Sim?' Geoffrey said. 'What's your story?'

'They're lying! I wouldn't lay a finger on Master Fletcher! Why should I?' Jack spat loudly, and Sim looked away as he saw that sardonic glance from the old bowman. 'Owen and I were out after deer. These two went for us. We didn't have a chance. Poor Owen had a shaft through his guts from young Nick here, and Master Fletcher nearly broke my nose. Plain murder it was!'

There was silence. The hard, brown faces of the six men who formed the court examined Sim, and he looked away. But everywhere he glanced, he saw the same grim faces of the other outlaws watching him. But no one spoke. They waited for Geoffrey.

'What arms were you carrying, Sim?' Geoffrey asked quietly.

Sim hesitated for a moment. 'A dagger,' he said.

'And Owen?'

'He had a dagger, too.'

Jack laughed hoarsely. He had not got Geoffrey's quickness of brain, but he was intelligent enough.

'And what sort of deer would you two catch with daggers?' he asked. 'A tame one that would come up and ask you to stick a perishing dagger into him?'

A roar of laughter went up from the outlaws, and Sim scowled at Geoffrey as he realized the trap into which he had walked.

'We wouldn't have hurt Master Fletcher,' he said. 'I had a score to settle with him. Fair fight it would have been if young Nick hadn't put a shaft through poor Owen.'

Silence fell on the court. Geoffrey looked at them and they nodded.

'You first, Jack,' he said.

'String him up, Geoffrey.'

'Yes,' the others said in turn.

'No! No!' Sim screeched. He struggled to free his hands, and turned this way and that, searching desperately for one friendly face. But every man looked at him with a chilly contempt and dislike. He flung himself on his knees, but Geoffrey's face was set, and Jack spat and turned his head away.

'You will hang in the morning,' Geoffrey said. 'Piers! Wat! Tie him up in that empty hut, and keep a watch on him.'

It was a cold night with a wind from the east, and the sky had been a dull leaden colour as the sun set. There would be snow before the end of the week, Hugh thought as he rolled himself in his blankets.

He awoke as a hand shook his shoulder. A cold wind was blowing into the hut through the open door, and someone was standing there with a torch spluttering in his hand.

'Hugh! Wake up!' It was Geoffrey speaking. 'Sim has escaped!'

Hugh crawled out unwillingly, and shivered.

'He's knifed Piers,' Jack said. 'He's dead.'

Hugh went to the door and looked out into the cold night.

'Snowing hard,' he said. 'We'll never follow his tracks now.'

'Let's hope he freezes to death in the forest,' Jack said. 'Serve the perisher right, and save us the trouble of hanging him.'

The snow had stopped falling when Hugh awoke again in the morning. It was a still day with a hard blue sky, and there were a couple of inches of snow on the ground, with deep drifts against the walls of the gorge. Every tree and bush carried its load of snow, glistening and sparkling in the sunlight. It was a pretty sight, Hugh supposed, but he disliked it; they would be kept close to the gorge for a few days, and it seemed that it might be longer than that, for it snowed again the next day. It was ten days later that Hugh set out for Fingle Cross to fetch his new bow, and he was not allowed to go alone this time. Nick and Jack insisted on coming with him, and Geoffrey stirred himself lazily by the fire, and said he would join them.

They went on horseback, muffled against the cold in thick hose and woollen undershirts, with a tunic and a heavy chaperon over their shoulders. They carried swords and daggers and bows, and if they were stopped by any curious officials on the roads, they would claim to be mounted bowmen in the service of Sir Henry Mortimer, a trick that made Jack chuckle hoarsely.

Sir Henry was still in France, so their informants in Goodrich had told them, but as an additional precaution they carried letters giving their names and occupations. The government had issued orders that all people travelling from town to town must carry some such document, hoping in this way to check the runaway serfs and villeins, and also the robbers and vagrants. Geoffrey had written the letters in his clerkly hand, and had even made a very reasonable copy of Sir Henry's signature, taken from a document he had been shown at Goodrich.

They rode into Fingle Cross at noon, and stabled the horses at the inn. They were cold and hungry after their ride, and went inside to roast themselves in front of the huge log-fire. The innkeeper greeted them respectfully; the outlaws who visited his inn always paid their way, for it was one of the strict rules that Hugh had laid down for their safety. There were

some other guests there, the inevitable pedlars, three merchants from Skenfrith, and the reeve from a neighbouring village. They glanced up at the outlaws, and went on with their meal. They knew who Hugh was, and his companions, and they had no quarrel with them. Indeed, they owed much to his ruthless discipline, for the roads around the forest were remarkably clear of robbers.

The door opened, and a burly, red-faced man stamped into the room. He made for the fire, and shouted to the landlord. He wore a sword, and carried a large leather wallet. A messenger, Hugh supposed, taking letters and other documents for some lord or bishop, but he seemed full of importance, and a stranger to the area. The innkeeper hurried up with a cup of wine, and the man stared about him as he drank. He ignored the obvious pedlars and the merchants, but he looked curiously and then suspiciously at the outlaws, who were sitting down now, and eating their meal. He stalked over to them.

'Your letters of travel,' he said curtly, and held out his hand.

Hugh looked up in surprise. The conversation from the other tables ended abruptly, and the clatter of knives ceased abruptly. The innkeeper had turned and was watching anxiously.

'What business is this of yours?' Hugh asked.

'I am in the service of the Earl of Northampton. I am his personal messenger.'

'Then deliver your messages, and leave us alone.' Hugh picked up his knife, and for the first time the Earl's messenger was conscious of the unnatural silence in the inn. He turned his head and saw the staring faces, and the innkeeper who had come to the table. Startled and uneasy he looked down at Hugh, and realized somewhat belatedly the formidable appearance of this young man. There was something very strange here, he thought, these men he had questioned, and very odd, too, was the attitude of the other travellers.

'I can vouch for these men,' the innkeeper said. 'We all know them here, sir.'

'Oh, I see,' the Earl's messenger said slowly. He went to a table and sat down, though he was not at all certain what it was he had seen. But he felt that he was well out of an awkward situation, and he ate his food in silence, keeping his eyes off those men with the swords and great bows.

Watkyn was glueing a new grip to a bow when they walked into his workshop. He put down his tools, smiled with pleasure when he saw Jack, and then took a bow from a rack.

'Here is your bow, Master Fletcher,' he said. There was a note of pride in his voice, and he stood back, his face crinkling with a quiet delight.

Hugh took the bow, and his eyes gleamed. At first sight the bow seemed too long for him, but he held it out in his left hand until the grip was on a level with his jaw. The length was right, and he knew that this was the longest bow he had ever used. The wood was dark and beautifully planed, so that the surface, as he passed his fingers over it, felt as smooth and hard as a piece of burnished steel. The back was flat, but the belly of the bow had a gracefully cut arch; each limb was thick and straight, and the tips had been covered with horn, each notched to hold the string. Even such details as the binding and the grip were finished with painstaking care and skill. This, Hugh saw, was the product of a master craftsman, and he smiled at the old bowyer.

'Yes, it is a fine bow,' Watkyn said. 'And you will find it so when you use it, Master Fletcher. But such a bow needs a good string. Flemish hemp is the best, and here it is.'

Hugh took the string, and let it run through his fingers. Flemish hemp was the most expensive string of all, and lasted longer than any other. He slipped one loop over the lower tip of the bow. The method of bracing a bow with its string was often called 'treading the bow', for it was best done with foot and hand working together. He put his left foot on the lower tip, and pressed outwards on the leather strip of the grip, forcing the bow to bend with the weight of foot and hand on the upper limb. As the bow arched, he slipped the other loop of the string into the upper nock.

He had made it appear a simple operation. But it was an easy matter to pinch your finger painfully between the string and the bow, and at some time in his life every bowman had done that, dancing with the pain as he sucked his fingers, while his friends laughed and stamped their feet with delight.

Hugh paid Watkyn, listening to his advice on waxing the bow, and keeping the wood supple. Damp was the great enemy of a long-bow, and of the string, too, for that matter.

Back at the gorge, Geoffrey and Jack examined the new bow with great and expert care, but Hugh had already made up his mind, though he knew that the real test would be at the butts.

'It's a sweet bow, Hugh,' Jack said. 'And here's something I made for you, though it's little repayment for what you did for me at Goodrich.'

He gave Hugh a long, narrow case of soft leather which he had been working at unnoticed by Hugh. He was skilled with his hands, and at leatherwork, and Hugh fitted the bow into it, and looked at Jack. But Jack, as if ashamed by his own generosity, had gone to collect the outlaws, and to lead them out to the butts.

The butts were half a mile from the gorge, placed at the end of a long piece of open ground, with trees on either side. The boys from the camp ran to the farther end to mark the fall of the shafts, while the outlaws stamped their feet on the frozen ground and beat their hands against their sides. Their breath hung in the air in clouds of steam, for though the sun was shining from a clear sky there was no warmth in the forest. Over the gorge the smoke from the fires rose in straight lines, and the trees were bare and still. The snow lay evenly over the ground and the coloured chaperons of the men were vivid splashes of red and yellow and blue against the background of dazzling white.

'Try a long cast at full range,' Jack said.

It was sound advice, for Hugh had no idea of the power of the new bow. He drew on a leather bracer as a protection for his left arm against the whip of the string, and picked out a dozen shafts that he had made himself, all with smooth, armour-piercing war-heads, and pushed them into the ground at his feet.

He knew this range well, of course, for he had loosed many hundreds of shafts here. His longest cast had fallen in line with an ancient oak that stood towards the end of the glade, and that had been with a following wind. But there was no breeze today, and he could give the bow a fair trial.

'Fast!' Nick yelled, and all the men took up the bowman's cry of warning. 'Fast! Fast!' The boys in the distance waved their arms and scurried away into the safety of the trees. Shafts were valuable, for they represented hours of patient work in the making, and any boy who missed the fall of one would probably be sore for days, so they crouched down on hands and knees, their eyes on the ground in front.

'Lay the body well into it, Hugh,' Geoffrey said.

Hugh nodded. No man could draw a bow such as this by brute strength alone, and Geoffrey, with his own colossal muscles, knew that better than most. Carefully Hugh nocked the first shaft and drew a long breath, filling his lungs with the cold, clear air of the forest. Then he began to draw, steadily and smoothly, the strain on his left hand and wrist, and the muscles of shoulder and back, his feet wide apart and pressing down on the frozen turf. And it was then the great bow came to life between his hands.

He felt, as he always did when he drew a long-bow, a sense of expectancy and exhilaration with the enormous power that lay in his grip. The tough Flemish string was nearly at full stretch, tugging back the thick limbs of the bow into a graceful arc, the feathers close to his ear, and his strong fingers on the cord. The bow was vibrant with pent-up energy and a suppressed sense of violent force greater than anything he had experienced before, and yet all of it was controlled by the delicate touch of the fingers of his right hand.

Gradually he relaxed their grip on the string. With a deep and exultant twang the great bow exploded with a furious blast of power as it unleashed its strength, hurling the thin shaft up into the blue sky. Hugh lowered the bow and sighed with contentment, head back, watching the shaft soar to the top of its flight, its speed at first almost too great for the eye to follow, and then slowing gradually, black against the sky, and black again as it swooped down towards the snow.

'Beyond!' Nick yelped. 'Twenty paces beyond the oak, Hugh!' And he jumped up and down, clapping his hands.

Two boys had raced out from the trees, halting by the shaft, while one of them pulled it out with care. If he broke it, and shafts with war-heads embedded themselves deeply into the ground, even frozen as it was today, he would feel Jack's cane when they returned to the gorge.

'You can do better than that,' Jack growled. He had been watching Hugh's fingers on the string. 'The shaft crept.'

Hugh grinned. Jack was right. He always was in matters of archery, and he could detect the slightest fault in a bowman's work. Hugh had been surprised by the power of the bow, and he had held his aim with the string at full stretch for a fraction of a second. The string, trying to resist the enormous strain of the thick limbs of the bow, had crept forward just before he had loosed. Both the velocity and the range of the shaft would be affected, the difference perhaps between it driving through the armour of a man or bouncing harmlessly away. The remedy, as Hugh well knew, was to increase the tension of the fingers, but then there was a danger of snatching or plucking, and the aim would suffer.

He nocked and drew again. Once more he felt the great surge of power between his hands as he loosed. The boys were already running out as the shaft came down, waving their hands as they turned towards the end of the range.

'Beyond!' Geoffrey said. Jack grunted and spat, a spit of satisfaction Hugh thought. But the length of a cast was not everything; accuracy at that range was what mattered.

'Try at the butts,' Jack said.

'Fast!' Nick yelled, and the others took up the cry.

The bales of straw that were used as targets were about half-way up the clearing, two hundred paces away perhaps, with patches of white cloth in the centre of each. Hugh nocked, and aimed at one butt in the centre. He waited to watch the fall of the shaft, and shook his head.

'Over,' Jack muttered. 'Well over. That's a stronger bow than you've ever used before, Hugh.'

Hugh loosed again, shortening the range. Again he was over, but only by a little. The third shaft landed full on the white clout, and he heard Jack's grunt of approval. As he saw it land, Hugh was nocking again. He drew and loosed and without a pause went through his swift, precise drill, nocking, drawing, loosing, until there was a steady trail of thin black shafts in the air, rising high above the level of the trees, swooping down towards the straw bales.

'He! He!' the outlaws shouted as the fourth shaft plunged down to follow the others that had already hit the white rag. Geoffrey nodded gravely, and Jack patted Hugh on the arm.

'Well, you're a master bowman now, Hugh,' he said. 'As smooth and sweet as ever I've seen.'

7

THE TOURNAMENT AT SKENFRITH

Nick came riding into the gorge at a gallop, and pulled up by the pool. He waved to Hugh, who was sitting outside his hut with Jack and Geoffrey, and dismounted with his usual haste for he never did anything slowly, and ran towards them.

'Nick's made a huge profit on the horses,' Geoffrey said.

'Or else he's lost them all,' Jack added.

'Nick's always excited,' Hugh said. 'It's nothing much, I expect.'

'I sold all six horses, Hugh!' Nick cried, and threw himself down on the ground beside Hugh. 'Good price, too. Exactly what you told me!'

'Well done, Nick. Any other news from Skenfrith?'

'The King's raising an army to go to France. That's what they said in the square. He wants several thousand knights and men-at-arms, and about ten thousand good bowmen.'

Geoffrey shrugged his broad shoulders, uninterested in the news. But Jack's eyes gleamed, and he plied Nick with questions, one finger rubbing the faded scar across his forehead. Geoffrey watched him for a moment, smiling, and then saw Hugh's face, and the smile vanished. Geoffrey knew all Hugh's moods so well, and he noticed the fists clenching and unclenching again, a sure sign that Hugh was stirred by some emotion.

'There's to be a big tournament at Skenfrith the Sunday after Easter,' Nick said. 'And after that a special contest for bowmen. A noble for every man who satisfies the judges, and ten for the winner.'

Jack growled and spat impatiently. 'Who'll be the judges?' he demanded. 'That's what matters. And what will satisfy them?'

'Someone told me that the captain of the King's Bowmen will be there. I didn't catch all the names. I was trying to sell one of the horses. It was someone called Giles.'

'Giles Allerton!' Jack exclaimed.

'Do you know him, Jack?' Nick asked.

'I was in Normandy with him years ago. We were in the same company of bowmen. Well, Giles will know how to pick out good bowmen.'

'And one of the men-at-arms from the castle said that Sir John Carey would be there with this man Giles.'

They all nodded, for this was a name that they knew. When people spoke of the King's commanders, the names of Sir John Chandos, Sir Walter Manney, and Sir John Carey were invariably mentioned, and in the towns and villages around the forest that of Carey was the best known, for he had a small manor at Grosmont, though he did not often visit it. His lands were in South Wales and in the Marches.

'I know Sir John, too,' Jack said. 'Served under him in Normandy. And I would again if I had to. He looks after his men.'

Hugh stirred, and Geoffrey glanced at his intent face.

'What about the conditions of the contest for bowmen?' Jack asked.

'They'll have to loose at not less than two hundred paces, and at straw figures the height of a horse and his rider. Each man to be given the same time, and to loose as many shafts as he can.'

'Sir John and Giles know what they're looking for,' Jack grunted. 'That'll separate the men from the boys.'

'Jack, you and Hugh could beat anyone!' Nick exclaimed.

'I might,' Jack said, 'if I were ten years younger. But Hugh could.'

Hugh shook his head, but Geoffrey thought he spoke reluctantly. 'Too risky,' he said. 'We're well known in Skenfrith.'

'There's not a man there who would give you away,' Nick said. 'You could give another name if you were asked.'

'I would like to see the tournament,' Hugh said slowly. 'Would you two come with us?'

'I will,' Geoffrey said instantly.

'And I!' Jack said. 'But Giles Allerton would recognize me. I'd have to keep out of his way.'

'And you'll enter the bowmen's contest?' Nick asked eagerly.

'Perhaps, Nick. I doubt it, though. Is Sir Henry Mortimer

at Goodrich? If he is, he'll be at the tournament, and if he sees us, we'll be in the dungeons of the castle before the end of the day.'

'I can find out,' Nick said. 'I know some of the villeins at Goodrich.'

During the next three weeks Hugh did not mention the tournament again, but he spent a good deal of his time on the range with his new bow. Perhaps there was no special significance in that, Geoffrey thought, but he noticed that Hugh was concentrating on speed of fire, and at a range of never less than two hundred paces. That, too, could mean nothing. As Jack had always insisted whenever he trained the outlaws, speed was the first essential, once the hard, grinding practice at drawing and loosing had been mastered; the ability to send off a steady stream of shafts with the certainty of hitting man or horse at two hundred paces would mean the difference between life and death in battle, he had often said. A competent bowman should be able to do that at half the range, but only the few, the real master bowmen, were consistently accurate at full range.

But one day Geoffrey saw Hugh laying out on the ground his collection of shafts with war-heads. He examined them all carefully, squinting down the shaft for any signs of warping that might effect the flight, testing the feathers, trimming them, and glueing on many new ones. Finally he set aside two dozen that satisfied his high standards, and packed them away in his quiver. He looked up suddenly to see Geoffrey watching him, and flushed, but he gave no explanation, and Geoffrey walked away thoughtfully. He had noticed Hugh's growing restlessness for some months, and he knew the reason.

The next day Nick was sent to Goodrich to question the people there, and came back with the news that Sir Henry was not at his castle, and was not expected there. He was still in France, so the steward had said.

'We'll go to Skenfrith tomorrow,' Hugh said. 'There'll be a lot of people there, and we can sell some of the best horses. We'll take a dozen. Jack, Geoffrey, Nick, you'll come?' They nodded. 'And Walter, Hal, and young Robert can help with the horses.'

'Weapons?' Jack asked.

'No swords. We don't want to look conspicuous.'

'What about bows?' Nick asked anxiously. He felt naked without his long-bow.

'Yes, bows. But keep them in their cases. Pack the quivers in the saddle-bags. We must look like honest freemen from the south of the forest. The Skenfrith people will know who we are, but they'll keep quiet.'

They rode for Skenfrith at dawn, a journey of about fifteen miles, on a warm morning in early spring, the forest green and fresh, and Hugh rode fast as if he were anxious to leave the forest behind him.

Skenfrith was not a large town, but it was the nearest market of any size, and the natural centre for all the villages and manors scattered around the forest. The road from the west was unusually crowded that morning; there were the inevitable pedlars and merchants, two troupes of acrobats and jugglers, a band of wandering musicians, many beggars and vagrants, and hundreds of men, women, and children from all the villages. A tournament was a great and exciting event in their monotonous lives, an excuse to leave their strips in the huge open fields, and to visit the town of Skenfrith, the farthest that most of them had ever travelled from their homes.

Among those on foot Hugh saw many men with long-bows, intent on entering for the archery contest, he supposed, and there were occasional groups of people on horseback, knights and squires, their ladies and grooms and servants, behind them the great horses on which they would ride in the tilting, and wagons loaded with tents, beds, food, and their armour, for there would be little room to spare in the castle of Skenfrith, or at the two inns.

A mile from the town they passed the gates of the great Cistercian monastery; the deep notes of a single bell came from the tower of the Abbey Church, and the white-robed monks and novices were filing in through the gates from the fields where they had been working.

The tournament itself was to be held outside the walls of Skenfrith, and a small tented town had already sprung up on the open space there, with lines of stalls where the shopkeepers and pedlars and merchants were laying out their goods. After the quiet of the forest, this place was a seething bedlam of noise. Apprentices were bellowing at passers-by, enticing them into their masters' shops, or plucking at their sleeves with their shouts of 'What do you lack?' Two men were banging huge drums by the booth where the jugglers were about to begin their first performance, and a little farther away the troupe of musicians and singers had already started. Children ran amidst the shifting, restless crowds, shrieking excitedly, and then the whole crowd scattered suddenly with yells of alarm as a tame bear was led along the stalls.

An open strip of ground, long and narrow, had been cleared for the jousting and the archery, marked off by stakes and ropes. At either end were the tents of the knights and squires, with their banners on long poles; along one side, nearest the walls of the town, a low wooden platform had been built, with benches and a few high-backed chairs for the most important visitors. Two standards hung there, one with a device of red bars, the arms of Sir Humphrey Clifford, who was the seneschal of Skenfrith Castle, a royal manor, and who held it for the King. The other banner bore the figure of a black hawk with outstretched wings, and was new to Hugh. He turned to Jack, who was familiar with the arms of the foremost soldiers of the day.

'The black hawk of the Careys,' Jack said. 'That's Sir John Carey's banner.' He spat. 'I've marched for many miles behind that standard.'

Hugh went away to find Nick, who was already bargaining with a possible buyer of one of the horses. Hugh did not interfere, for Nick was a shrewd and experienced seller of horses, and he would sell all twelve that day, Hugh thought, and at high prices.

A trumpet blew from the lists, and the heralds in their coloured jupons marched out to announce the first bouts. These were between squires, and Hugh, after watching the first three pairs ride against each other, went back again to the horses. The most exciting and skilled part of the jousting would come later in the day when the more experienced knights would be riding. He found Jack sitting on the ground behind the horses.

'I thought you would be watching the jousting?' Hugh said.

'Too many of my old friends here,' Jack said. 'Giles Allerton is here, right enough. I saw him by the dais, and there's half a dozen more bowmen of the King's Company with him. I know three of 'em.'

The jousting went on throughout the morning, and for the best part of the afternoon, and when the last bout had finished, the heralds marched out again, and the trumpets blew for silence.

'All bowmen wishing to enter the archery contest to report at the end of the lists!' they bellowed, and walking down to the other end, they repeated the notice.

'You, Hugh?' Jack muttered.

'Perhaps. I'll see what the others do.' Instinctively he was following the rule of the forest, to wait and watch before making a move.

There were at least a hundred bowmen gathering at the end of the lists, and standing in front of them were two men. One was a nobleman, in jupon and hose, with sword and dagger at his waist, about thirty-five years of age, Hugh thought, brown-haired and clean-shaven. His features were sharp and pointed, a pleasant looking man, intelligent and alert.

'Sir John Carey,' Jack said. 'And that's Giles Allerton with him.'

Giles might have been a replica of Jack. He wore a brigandine and steel helmet, sword and dagger, his equipment highly burnished, and all of it spotless and neat. His skin was burnt to a deep brown by the sun, his expression hard and watchful, and though he was well built, there was no fat, only a tough and wiry strength that marked the veteran soldier.

'Pay attention, if you please,' Sir John called out in a clear, somewhat high-pitched voice. There was instant silence.

'Always courteous,' Jack whispered. 'He speaks to king or bowman alike.'

Hugh looked at the famous soldier with a new interest. Behind that simple request for silence was an effortless air of confidence, and quiet though the voice had been, the effect had been immediate. Here, Hugh knew, was a natural leader of men, and with a method so very different from the chilly menace of Sir Henry Mortimer, or his own abrupt and often ruthless ways with the outlaws.

'The conditions are these,' Sir John said. 'You will loose ten at a time, each at his own target down there,' and he pointed to the far end of the lists where men were setting up tall bales of straw, crudely shaped to represent the height and appearance of a man on horseback, and at a distance that Hugh estimated must be nearly two hundred paces.

'When the trumpet sounds, you may start to draw, but not before, and you must not touch your first shaft until then. No shafts to be loosed after the trumpet sounds again. The heralds will take your names, and record your hits. Giles, will you fall in the first ten bowmen.'

'What name will you give?' Jack asked.

'Wait,' Hugh said. There were several among the bowmen who had glanced at him, and then away again; they knew who he was, but they would say nothing.

'Your name?' one of the heralds asked him.

'Roger Bowyer of Fingle Cross.'

The herald did not even look at him, and scratched the name down on his parchment, before passing on to the next man. As Giles Allerton drew up the first ten bowmen in line, the crowd hummed with interest. These were their friends and relations waiting to loose, and each bowman had brought with him a large group of supporters from his village. The trumpet blew and they began to loose with a desperate haste.

'You can beat these fumbling perishers with your eyes shut,' Jack grumbled to Hugh after three lots of men had finished. 'Look at 'em! Plucking at the string like frightened boys, letting the shafts creep, bad grips . . . why, there's one fool who's dropped a shaft! I bet Giles is saying a few choice words under his breath.'

Hugh grinned, though Jack was right enough. Most of the bowmen there were indifferent by the high standards of the forest. But when Hugh turned to speak to him, the old fellow had vanished in the crowd. Giles Allerton had just moved across to that side of the lists, and was standing quite close to Hugh, talking to Sir John Carey.

'Well, Giles?' Sir John said.

'Not well, my lord. Few good bowmen here.'

They stood there until nearly all had loosed, and then Hugh heard his name being called, or rather the name he had given to the herald.

'Only one left, Giles,' Sir John said. 'You loose with this man, and show these people how a long-bow should be used.'

Hugh walked forward. To his dismay he saw that he had waited too long, and he could not have made himself more conspicuous, for only Giles and himself were standing on the line. But he could not draw back now, and methodically he made his preparations. He emptied his quiver of the two dozen shafts he had brought with him, all picked with great care, as Geoffrey had guessed, and pushed the war-heads into the turf, with the cock feathers pointing in the same direction so that they would come to hand without any need to fumble or hesitate when nocking. He adjusted the leather bracer on his arm, and took his stance, looking for an aiming mark. He had decided on his plan, after watching the other bowmen: they had loosed wildly once the trumpet had blown, hoping to correct their aim and the range as they went. The results had been indifferent, as Giles Allerton had said, and the highest number of hits so far had been eight. But Hugh was determined to watch the flight of his first shaft before he even began to draw for the second. Once he was certain of the range, and only then, would he loose and draw with all the tremendous speed of which he was capable.

The crowd was humming with excitement. A group of the King's Bowmen were shouting raucous encouragement to Giles, and their remarks on the ability of those who had already loosed, and on this tall young rustic villager who stood on the mark beside Giles, were rude and amusing. The local people laughed, too, for by this time the real name of the young man had been passed around in whispers, and there was not a person who lived within twenty miles of the great forest who had not heard of Hugh Fletcher.

Sir John glanced at Giles, who nodded, and one of the heralds raised his trumpet. The roar of voices died away, and for a brief moment there was a dead silence, broken suddenly by the shrill blast of the trumpet.

Hugh snatched up a shaft. He nocked and drew, his left hand clamped like a piece of steel on the grip of his great bow. Up came arm and bow, until his knuckles were on a line with a pennant flying at the far end of the lists, and he loosed.

Pressed against the ropes a few yards away was Jack, his eyes on the two bowmen. He was one of the few there who noticed that Hugh had loosed before Giles Allerton, and he nodded and spat. But Sir John had noticed, too, and his sharp-featured and intelligent face was intent as he watched Hugh.

Hugh picked up his next shaft, glanced for a brief moment at the cock feather, put it to the string, and then waited for his first shaft to fall. He saw it swoop down and there were the feathers quivering at the very top of the target. He grinned. He had not expected such luck for that first cast. He drew again lowering his aim a fraction, and loosed. There was no pause this time. He nocked immediately and began to draw, and then in rapid succession he went through his drill. The bowmen who were watching gasped and nudged each other. They might not be master bowmen, but they knew what years of hard and patient practice were needed to attain such an effortless skill. The great bow that Watkyn had made, bent and straightened; the tough Flemish string twanged exultantly, and hurled a steady stream of shafts away, an unending and graceful curve, up into the blue sky and the white clouds that drifted overhead, pausing for a moment, it seemed, at the highest point, and then curving down again towards the tall bale of straw.

The crowd at that end of the lists began to roar and hands were being waved. The King's Bowmen had fallen silent. They were real bowmen, and they knew what they were watching was an exhibition of such skill as they had never witnessed before. The trumpet blared out above the clamour of the crowd, and Hugh stood there, head up, his eyes on his last shaft as it plunged down into the heart of the target. His breathing was a little faster after his tremendous exertions, for no man could draw a long-bow without a vast expenditure of energy, but he could have gone on for another two dozen casts at least without a rest.

He looked down to see how many shafts were left out of the twenty-four he had set out. There were five left. He marched down the lists towards his target, and from the people packed against the ropes he heard the bellowed shouts of delight. Sir John Carey walked down, too, and his face was expressionless, but his shrewd eyes were twinkling with amusement. For even at that distance it was possible to see the feathers in the two targets.

'Twelve for Master Allerton, my lord,' a herald said.

'My lord, my lord!' another was shouting. 'There are seventeen in this target!'

'Seventeen!' Giles said. 'Are you certain, man?'

'Yes, Master Allerton. See for yourself.'

'Well, Giles?' Sir John asked quietly.

Master Allerton's hard brown face was set and angry, and then he laughed, showing a row of yellow teeth. 'Oh, I give him best, my lord.'

'Your name?' Sir John asked Hugh.

'Roger Bowyer, my lord.'

'And what are you?'

'I come from Fingle Cross, my lord. My father is a master bowyer, and I am his apprentice.' Hugh told the tale glibly and without any hestitation. He knew that old Watkyn would never contradict anyone who questioned him about it, for Hugh had paid him many visits in the winter months, and they were close friends now. Nor would anyone in Fingle Cross dispute the fact that Watkyn had a son called Roger, if they were asked. Hugh Fletcher's band were a peaceful enough lot of men, but no one wished to make enemies of them.

Sir John inspected Hugh from head to foot, the slow appraising inspection of an experienced commander of men, who knew that in the last resort he must depend upon the qualities and morale of those he led into battle.

'I am raising a company of bowmen to march with me to France,' he said. 'You can be their captain, if you wish.'

Hugh's eyes gleamed, and then he hesitated. 'I would talk first with my father, my lord.'

'Do so, Master Bowyer. I shall be at Grosmont for two weeks at least. Bring me your answer there.' He smiled at Hugh in a friendly way, and Hugh's stern face relaxed. He liked this man, he decided. He had been attracted by him when Jack had first pointed him out.

'I will, my lord,' he said, and bowed and smiled.

'Let me see that bow of yours, boy,' Giles said. He ran his

brown fingers over the smooth wood, peered at the grain and the finish of the weapon, and he nodded.

'You made this?'

'My father.'

'I wish he would make one like it for me.'

Sir John was watching them. 'I think, Giles, that you would have found it difficult to match this young man in your younger days.'

Giles shrugged his shoulders. 'I must be honest, my lord. I doubt if I could have, even then. And I would say that about two other bowmen only, men I marched with in Normandy, Robert Miller, who was killed at Caen, and Jack Cherryman, and I know not what happened to him.'

'Then I will see you, Master Bowyer, when the prizes are given,' Sir John said, 'and later, I hope, at Grosmont.' He nodded with the same charming and friendly smile, and strolled away.

But when the heralds called out the name of Roger Bowyer of Fingle Cross an hour later, no one stepped forward to receive the bag of nobles as the winner of the contest for bowmen. Many men in the crowd smiled and nudged their neighbours, and Sir John, alone of those on the dais, noticed the slight gestures, and the suppressed smiles. He tugged at his pointed chin, his face puzzled.

As for Hugh, he was ten miles away, riding hard for the forest, silent and thoughtful. Nick and Jack were crowing with delight at his success, and wondered at his apparent lack of enthusiasm. But Geoffrey said nothing. He knew. The time had come, he guessed, for Hugh to leave the forest, and he was wondering what he himself would do when that time arrived for certain, and Hugh made his decision.

8

SIR JOHN CAREY

Hugh sat with his back against a tree, and stared down at the white strip of the road below him. He was by himself, as he often was now in the days following the tournament at Skenfrith. For Geoffrey had been right, and Hugh knew that he could not stay much longer in the forest. He had done what he had wished to do, to organize the outlaws into a disciplined and prosperous community, and he had made himself their undisputed leader. That experience of power and authority had been exhilarating, but there was no more to be done now, except continue the same monotonous succession of winter, spring, summer, and then winter again, in the depths of the forest.

Outside was a world about which he knew nothing. But he did know that there would be something new for him there, and Sir John Carey's offer had given him a chance to start an entirely new life. But his instinctive caution had made him hesitate. For several days now he had left the gorge, and wandered about the forest, trying to make up his mind. He smiled, for he was never entirely alone. Since that attempt by Sim to murder him, Nick and the other outlaws followed him at a distance. Hugh was not supposed to know that. But he was too good a forester not to know when he was being followed, though he had not told Nick so. The outlaws were not far away now, he thought. He had heard their whistles and signals.

The road was empty at the moment. Half an hour ago Hugh had watched a long procession of cattle on their way to London from Wales, with their drovers in their wide-brimmed hats and homespun coats, and their strange cries in Welsh.

Hugh sat up and looked across the road. He thought he had heard voices, but there was no one to be seen. He rolled over and crept forward through the long grass. On the other side of the road was the open moorland, with some bushes and an occasional tree. The voices came from the direction of the bushes, he thought. One of them moved. But there was no wind, so why should it shake like that? Then he saw the shape of a man's head, and to the left were two more men. Robbers, of course, he guessed. No honest men would lie hidden there by the side of the main road from Skenfrith. They could not be from the gorge. Hugh's mouth set grimly. If they were, they would regret it.

He crawled back slowly to the trees where he could stand without being seen. He had left his bow there, and his quiver, and he took out half a dozen shafts. They were hunting-broad-heads, but they would be effective enough against the robbers, even if they wore mail shirts, for the range would be short. Then he settled down to wait with the grim and stubborn patience of the trained hunter.

He raised his head. In the distance he had heard the clip-clop of hooves coming from the right. The road curved away behind the trees at this point, so he could not see the riders, for there was more than one horse, he thought.

The robbers must have heard the horses, too, for one of them jumped up and ran out on to the road from where he could see around the corner. He waved his arm, and ran back again to join his friends. Hugh frowned. He had seen that shuffling gait before, and that head hanging down on one side. Yes, it was Sim, the man who had murdered poor Piers, and who should have frozen to death in the snowstorm when he had escaped from the gorge. Hugh's hand went to his bow, and he stood up, shaft in his right hand, ready to nock and draw. Sim would not escape this time.

The horses were closer now, coming on a steady canter, and then they came around the corner, three of them. In front was a nobleman and a lady, gaily dressed both of them, the man in a yellow cotehardie, his blue mantle streaming behind him, a small velvet hat on his head, with a jaunty little feather. The lady was riding side-saddle, in blue and gold, and both of them were a tempting sight for any robbers. Behind them rode a man-at-arms, in steel helmet and mail shirt, and on the front of his white surcoat was the black figure of a hawk with out-stretched wings. But Hugh had not needed the sight of that, for he had recognized the nobleman immediately. It was Sir John Carey.

A bow twanged from the bushes. The shaft whistled across the road and hit Sir John's horse. It reared up so suddenly that he was thrown from the saddle. As he fell, another shaft swept over him. The lady cried out, and the man-at-arms crouched down in his saddle, and with a yell of alarm galloped furiously down the road in the direction from which he had just come.

Hugh ran forward. He had not expected the robbers to use bows. Sim had never handled one, so far as he could remember. And there was Sim, rushing out from his shelter, and the other two on each side of him, waving swords. They shouted, and saw in front of them a woman on a frightened horse, and a man lying, probably senseless, on the road. This was a simple and profitable little affair, and they came on gleefully, unaware of the dreadful menace of the single figure with the great bow standing up there under the trees.

Hugh was drawing, legs apart, shoulders square, his mouth a thin line, and his eyes half closed. There would be no mercy for those men now, and least of all for Sim. By the laws of the forest his life was already forfeit. He held his breath as his hand came back to his ear, the bow straining against the tug of the string, and his fingers relaxed. The shaft flew low over the slope and high across the road. It caught the right-hand man full in the chest and flung him backwards in an untidy and writhing heap. His brief and high-pitched scream of terror and pain brought the other two to a halt.

They had made a fatal mistake. To a master bowman such as Hugh a running target was not an impossible shot. But two stationary figures at that range meant sudden and certain death. He had nocked and was beginning to draw the second shaft before the first had hit its mark. He shifted his left hand round and loosed again. The man on Sim's right caught a brief glimpse of the thin shaft hurtling across the road and straight for him. He put out his hands in a futile gesture of defence, shrieked horribly, and went back, smashed to the ground by the frightful impact.

Sim shouted and turned to run, pounding at the ground with frantic haste and energy, running as he had never run before, head down and shoulders hunched, making for the three trees a hundred paces distant. Up came Hugh's left hand; he felt the tremendous pressure of the bow on the hardened muscles of his wrist, but his grip stayed firm and still, as solid and unyielding as the cliff that overlooked the gorge. The slim shaft lay ready, and Hugh loosed. He watched the blur of the grey feathers, the flicker of colour from the cock feather, the flight straight and true, streaking over the white road at a speed that baffled the eye, driven by the combined strength of the Flemish string and the thick limbs of the great bow. The broad head drove into Sim's back, on through the leather jerkin as if it had been paper, and flung him forward on his face. He did not even call out. He lay there motionless, the three feathers standing up horribly in his back as if in a dreadful signal of triumph, the signal of a silent and merciless death.

Sir John was on his feet, sword in hand, and he was holding the reins of the lady's horse. His own horse, not badly wounded, had bolted up the road and out of sight. Sir John had been looking over his shoulder towards the trees from where those three murderous shafts had come, but he remained quite unruffled, and was muttering soothing noises to the horse and the lady. But he dropped the reins as he saw a tall young man with fair, bleached hair walking slowly down the slope, a quiver and a sword at his belt, and a long bow in his left hand. As Sir John recognized that strong, set face, the arrogant curving nose, and

the forward thrust of the big chin, his eyes opened in surprise, and then he smiled.

'The bowman of Skenfrith,' he said, as Hugh stopped and bowed politely. 'I have a feeling, Master Bowyer, if that is indeed your name, that you are more than an apprentice from Fingle Cross. If you are, then you are a long way from your carpenter's bench.'

Hugh's smile broadened into a grin, for he was, after all, a very young man, and he found it difficult to remain the stern and aloof leader of a band of rough and numerous body of outlaws. Besides, he had taken a quick liking to Sir John, and his friendly manner, and the frequent gleam of amusement in those shrewd grey eyes.

'My name is Hugh Fletcher, my lord. You will not have heard . . .'

'Oh, I've heard of you, Master Fletcher. I came all the way from Wales to Grosmont to find you.'

'To find me!'

'Not to take a famous outlaw prisoner, Master Fletcher.'

'I should hope not, John,' the lady said decisively. 'He has just saved our lives.'

Sir John smiled at her. 'My wife, Master Fletcher. As you hear, I have to do as she orders.'

Hugh grinned, and bowed to the Lady Carey. She was a plump and comfortable looking lady, dark and handsome, with a kindly expression, and the same amused twinkle in her eyes as her husband. They seemed a happy and contented couple, Hugh thought.

'Well, that was not the reason why I came,' Sir John said. 'I had heard tales of you and your men from Sir William Assailly, who is my seneschal at Grosmont.'

They turned as a group of horsemen came galloping up the road. In the lead was a knight whom Hugh knew by sight, the Sir William that Sir John had just spoken of as his seneschal, and behind him were half a dozen men-at-arms, and a couple of young squires. Sir William was an elderly man, grey-bearded, with a red, choleric face, well known for his bursts of quick, excitable rage, and his sudden changes to genuine kindliness. He was well liked at Grosmont, so the outlaws had heard.

He dismounted, and ran across the road. 'You are unhurt, my lady?' he asked anxiously. 'And you, John? We stopped this gutless piece of horseflesh who came galloping up the road as if a French army was behind him.' He gestured contemptuously to the man-at-arms who had been riding with Sir John and Lady Carey.

'We are quite safe, William,' Sir John said.

'Killed the scoundrels, have you? And caught one of them, too,' he said, looking at Hugh. 'Robert, Edward, tie the fellow up!'

But the two men-at-arms had recognized Hugh. They glanced uneasily at Sir William, and hesitated. One of the other men, a stranger to the district, and who had come from Sir John's lands in Wales, moved forward.

'Wait, Gregory,' Sir John said. 'William, this is the man who killed the robbers and saved our lives. He is also the man you told me about. This is Hugh Fletcher.'

Sir William's face went even redder. 'So it is! Well, that's different,' he added hastily.

Sir John laughed. 'You puzzle me, Master Fletcher. You came out very boldly to speak to me. As the King's man, I should lay hands on you as an outlaw.'

'You would not take me far, my lord.'

'That's true enough, John,' Sir William said. 'I don't want a hundred master bowmen buzzing round the walls of Grosmont. You heard what happened at Goodrich.'

'I did. Sir Henry Mortimer has no love for you, Master Fletcher,' Sir John said.

'Nor I for him.'

'We are of one mind about that, then. But I am curious. Why are you so safe here?'

Hugh smiled and, turning his head, put his fingers to his mouth and whistled shrilly. There was a rustle from the trees, and Sir William swore loudly. Sir John began to laugh. Along the edge of the forest there had suddenly appeared a long line of men in dark-green jerkins and hose. Each carried a long-bow, and every man had a shaft on the string. Hugh waved his hand, and the bows came down.

'You are well served, Master Fletcher,' Sir John said, quite unmoved by this display of force that could have massacred every man in his small troop. 'I am all the more anxious to talk to you. Will you ride to Grosmont with me? I give you my knightly word that you may leave unharmed at any time you wish.'

'Yes, I will come, my lord,' Hugh said instantly.

'Then for heaven's sake tell those men of yours that you're in no danger!' Sir William said anxiously.

Hugh ran up the bank and spoke to Nick for a moment. His horse was tethered a little farther away in the forest, and he led it down to where Sir John was waiting.

'What about this fellow?' Sir William said, pointing to the man-at-arms who had run away and deserted Sir John and his wife. 'String him up, John, or take the skin off his back when we reach Grosmont?'

'If God made him a coward, William, then a flogging will not turn him into a brave man. Strip the brigandine and helmet off him, and turn him loose. I have no further use for him.'

Hugh nodded. His respect and liking for Sir John were increasing at every moment, and he rode towards Grosmont with his mind already quite clear about the decision he would make when they arrived.

Gosmont was not a large castle; it was a modest enough place with a small keep on a mound, and a low curtain wall with only the usual round towers at each corner, and on either side of the gatehouse. Hugh was led by one of the men-at-arms to a place at a table in the hall, for it was the time for the midday meal. Curious eyes watched him, and he was served with respect, for many knew him by sight, and all by reputation. When he had finished, Sir John and Sir William, followed by their squires and two young pages, went out to the bailey, and Hugh joined them there.

'The bowmen are practising at the butts,' Sir John said. 'I would like you to see them, Master Fletcher.'

'Where are they from, my lord?'

'Some are from here. Sir William has been training them. A few are old soldiers who have served with me in France. They are good bowmen. But the rest are not the equals of your men, from what I have heard.'

The butts had been set up on the far side of the dry ditch that surrounded the castle, and about thirty men were there, loosing at the straw targets. Sir John halted behind them, and in silence he watched the practice. Hugh walked up and down, his eyes on the bowmen's hands, intent on the little details that mattered, the grip of the fingers on bow and string, the steadiness of the draw, and the vital moment of release. As Sir John had said, there were some good bowmen there, but the rest needed several weeks of intensive training with a man like Jack in charge of them.

There was a pause as the bowmen came back with their shafts, and the white-haired man-at-arms, who was supervising the drill, came up to Sir John.

'My lord! The men would see Master Fletcher loose a few shafts, if he would.'

Sir John glanced inquiringly at Hugh, who nodded. The bowmen gathered around in a half circle, watching his preparations, as he braced his bow, pulled on a bracer, and pushed a dozen shafts into the ground. They had been loosing at targets at a range of a hundred paces, but beyond was a single bale, perhaps just under two hundred paces, Hugh thought, as he took up his stance, and nocked a shaft. He hesitated, and then pulled up a few blades of grass, throwing them in the air to test the strength and direction of the wind. There was a slight breeze from right to left, and he preferred that to a following wind. One shaft might well drift on for an extra twenty paces under such conditions, and the next drop as much short.

He loosed, and nocked again, but he waited for the fall of the first shaft. It came down just short, and unhurriedly he drew and loosed again, and once more he waited. The bowmen muttered as the second swooped down into the centre of the bale, and then they fell silent as Hugh began to draw and loose at full speed, their heads up watching the stream of shafts, ten in rapid succession, whistling away, up and then down, one after the other, following each other into the straw, until the last one landed, and the whole bale toppled over, riddled with the grey feathers.

'He! He!' they shouted, and waved their bows. Sir William whistled softly, and Sir John brought his hands together in one sharp crack.

'Robert, collect Master Fletcher's shafts for him,' he said. 'I would have a word with you, Master Fletcher.'

He walked through the gatehouse, across the bailey, and up the steps to the keep, down the full length of the hall, and through the door that opened into the solar, the private chamber of the lord of the castle. After the bare and bleak simplicity

of the hall, this was a small and comfortable room, with tapestries covering the stone walls and brightly coloured mats on the floor. On either side of the fire-place were two high-backed chairs, and Lady Carey was sitting in one of them, busy at a small loom, with many balls of wool of different colours on the table by her side.

Sir John stood with his back to the empty fire-place and waved a hand to one of the stools. Hugh bowed and sat down; it was a mark of considerable respect that he was asked to sit at all.

'Those robbers would have cut our throats this morning,' Sir John said. 'My wife and I are in your debt, Master Fletcher.'

'Please call me Hugh, my lord. That is what all my men call me.'

Sir John smiled. 'Very well, Hugh. There is one simple way of repaying you.' He picked up a small leather pouch, and handed it to Hugh. It clinked richly. 'So take that with my thanks.'

'Thank you, my lord.' Hugh waited, for there was much more to be said, he guessed.

'There is more I would like to do. This question of your outlawry, Hugh. What was your crime?'

'None, my lord.'

'None! Then how came you to the forest?'

Hugh repeated the story that he had once told Ambrose of Beverley.

'And your parents? What were they, Hugh?'

'I don't know, sir. Does it matter? I have made my own life.'

'You have done that, Hugh. But is it enough for you? I can offer you far more. With my help, and you will have that, you could go far.'

Hugh stiffened, and he looked eagerly at the knight. Here at last was the opportunity for which he had been waiting so restlessly during the last year, and the last, endless winter in the forest.

Sir John noticed the expression on his face, and nodded. 'Listen, Hugh. The King is taking an army to France. It may be Flanders, or even Normandy. But that is not my concern. The King will raise the army by granting Indentures to commanders such as myself, and he will pay us according to the number we bring. I shall have five knights and a dozen squires in my company. That is easy. I can make my pick from fifty who would follow my standard. But the campaign will be won, I believe, and the King agrees, by bowmen. I want a hundred and fifty good bowmen. I will make you their captain, if I can find the men!'

'Yes, my lord.'

'Yes? What do you mean, Hugh?'

I will be your Captain of Bowmen, my lord, and I will bring you about ninety master bowmen at least.'

Sir John laughed with glee, and clapped his hands together. He dropped into the other chair.

'That is why I came to Grosmont. I wanted your men.'

'They are outlaws, my lord.'

Sir John waved his hand as if to dismiss the problem. 'Once they march under my standard, they cease to be outlaws,' he said. 'But I must have good bowmen, and I must have discipline.'

Hugh half smiled as he thought of the discipline he had imposed upon the outlaws.

'Will you ride with me into the forest tomorrow, my lord? I will show you if they are bowmen, and you can see for yourself the state of their discipline.'

'Into the forest?' Lady Carey had been listening, and she looked up anxiously.

'I cannot give you anything but the word of an outlaw, my lady,' Hugh said. 'But I promise you that no harm will come to Sir John.'

'I will accept that, Hugh.' Sir John said. 'We will ride to the forest after dawn. I must confess that I am eager to see this famous camp of yours.'

They rode out from Grosmont a couple of hours after sunrise, and Sir John, as if anxious to show Hugh how much trust he put in his word, wore no armour, and came without his usual escort. As a further gesture, he allowed his young son, Philip, a boy of twelve, who had watched Hugh at the butts the previous day, to come with them.

They rode steadily for two hours through the great forest, and by that time Sir John confessed that he was hopelessly lost, and that he had little idea of which general direction he would have taken had he wished to ride back to Grosmont. They halted to water the horses at a stream, and some deer scampered away, to young Philip's delight.

'You could have hit them both, Master Fletcher?' he said. 'Quite easily, couldn't you?'

Hugh smiled. 'I am not sure of it, Master Philip,' he said.

'Wouldn't he have hit them, Father?'

'Of course, boy,' Sir John said. He was lying at his ease with his back against a tree, drinking from a flask of wine, for the day was warm, and they had eaten early that morning.

'Shall we go on, my lord?' Hugh asked.

'In half an hour, Hugh. It is very pleasant here. And I am sure that Philip will try to climb one of these trees. See that he doesn't break his neck. I promised his mother that that would not happen.'

They reached the ravine that led into the gorge an hour later, and there Hugh reined in with a gesture of warning. Sir John halted, and his thin face was alive with interest. From the trees ahead came a low whistle, and Hugh put his hands to his mouth, calling with the signal of recognition that he had taught the sentries. Two boys slid down a tree-trunk, and from behind another Nick appeared, bow in hand. Sir John made no comment, but he nodded. This was one of the things he had been looking for.

They rode into the gorge and dismounted, and Hugh led Sir John to his hut.

'This is Geoffrey of Cambridge, my lord,' he said. 'And this . . .'

Sir John was staring at Jack. 'I've seen you before,' he said. 'You're . . . now, let me think. That's it, Jack Cherryman!'

Jack grinned with pleasure. 'Yes, my lord. In Gascony it was.'

'A fine bowman, the best in the company, and the biggest looter, too.'

'That's right, too, my lord,' Jack said, and spat. He saw Philip looking up at him, and he winked. 'Your son, my lord?'

'Yes, Jack. But I didn't bring him here to learn any of your bad habits. Now, Hugh, will you tell your friends what I have in mind.'

Sir John sat on a stool outside the hut while Hugh called all the outlaws together. He told them briefly that Sir John wished to recruit them into a company of bowmen for the campaign in France. They would be mounted bowmen, and equipped at the King's expense, and they would receive a regular pay and rations, and their chance of loot and ransom money. Their outlawry would come to an end immediately. As for the older

men, the women and the children, they could remain in the gorge if they wished, under the protection of Sir John, acting through his seneschal, Sir William Assailly.

Hugh finished, and waited for the arguments. But there were none. He looked around in surprise. He was accustomed to a ready acceptance of his ideas, but this was startling. Geoffrey smiled.

'I told them last night that this was what you would suggest, Hugh,' he said. 'We've talked it over, and we are ready to follow Sir John.'

Jack spat. 'That's settled, then.'

'I have one condition, Master Cherryman,' Sir John said. 'I want to see what I am buying. Can these men of yours use their bows?'

'You can see for yourself, my lord,' Jack said. 'We are all ready.'

'Oh, are you?' Sir John said in surprise.

'Yes, my lord. If you would follow us to the butts.'

Jack winked at Hugh, and marched away. As they reached the long clearing Hugh saw that Jack had already set up a long line of targets at the far end, and he drew up the outlaws in position, until every man had sufficient room to draw and loose.

'Two hundred paces, my lord,' Jack said.

Sir John nodded. He stood at one end of the line, and watched the preparations closely. Much of his life had been spent in warfare, and by this time he could tell at a glance the type of men he was inspecting. These brown-faced, sturdy outlaws, stolid and well drilled, were the most promising soldiers he had seen for many years. If they could use their bows, then he would be a fortunate commander, he felt.

'How many men?' he asked.

'Ninety, my lord,' Geoffrey said.

'A dozen shafts apiece,' Jack said. He turned to the bowmen, who had all pushed their shafts into the ground and were waiting quietly, their eyes on Jack.

'Nock!' he shouted in his hoarse voice. 'Draw and loose!'

Up came the long line of bows, bending as they did so. Ninety shafts whistled away, but Sir John did not turn his head to watch them. His attention was on the bowmen as they nocked again. But there was no pause in the drill, swift, precise, and deadly. The air above the clearing was filled with the hordes of shafts, and there was no break in the thick, curving flight, as the strings twanged, and the arrows leapt away with a soft rustle and hiss. Then all the bows came down. The last shaft had gone, over a thousand in a matter of minutes.

Sir John nodded. Without a word he marched towards the targets, followed by all the others. He reached the end of the clearing, and in silence he strolled across the line of the straw bales. They were riddled with shafts, and the ground around, to a distance of a few yards, had sprouted a thick crop of feathers. If three lines of men had been drawn up there they would have been massacred. Hugh smiled. There could not have been a more convincing exhibition of what the long-bow could do in the hands of experts. A thousand or more shafts hurled at two hundred paces in a few minutes with a fearful accuracy was a feat that might well astonish the most experienced of soldiers.

'Well, my lord?' he said to Sir John.

'You have done your work well, all of you. I have not seen such fine bowmen before. When I march into France I will have the best company in the army behind my standard.'

9

THE GATHERING OF THE ARMY

Sir John Carey reined in by the side of the road to watch the column as it rode past. In the van were three of his knights and ten squires, all in mail and plate, for he had insisted that they must become accustomed now to the weight and discomfort of armour on a long march under a hot sun. One of the squires carried his personal standard with the black hawk, and another the forked pennant to show that Sir John was a Knight Banneret.

Hugh rode at the head of a hundred and fifty bowmen, all well mounted, and all equipped alike, in helmet, brigandine, sword, and dagger. The helmets covered the head and neck, but left the face exposed, and the brigandines were made of leather covered with small plates of steel. The long-bows were strapped to the saddle, and each man carried a quiver holding two dozen shafts.

At the rear were fifty spare horses, and then came the wagons, loaded with all the stores that experience had taught Sir John were so vital: food, wine, tents, boots, and clothing, and hundreds of bundles of arrow shafts, the life-blood of the bowmen. More knights and squires, pages and servants brought up the rear-guard, and Sir John nodded and smiled. He was content. This, he knew, was the best trained and most completely equipped company he had ever led to war.

He had concentrated his force at Grosmont. The knights and squires came mostly from the Marches of Wales, where Sir John's main lands lay, and the rest from the area of the forest of Goodrich. They were a carefully picked group of men, and Sir John could have brought many more. He was a famous and successful soldier, and there were many knights who wished to follow his banner. Some were genuine soldiers, others were new to battle; they were all attracted by the glory and the excitement of warfare, and the promise of loot and the prospect of an enormous ransom to be extracted from some rich French nobleman. Sir John's motives were somewhat different. He enjoyed leading men and tackling the problems of war; he was a rich man, and ransoms to him were not essential, though he was content enough to accept them. As for the glory of war, about which his younger knights and squires talked so much, he had very different views, but he never spoke of them.

Hugh was content with his new life. The forest now seemed almost like a prison, and he delighted in the changing scenes as they marched steadily towards the coast, over moorland and heath, past villages with their straggling streets of wattle and daub huts, the stone church and the manor house or castle, and the three huge open fields with the villeins crowding to the roadside to watch the column march past them.

He tried to keep his air of thoughtful silence and the stern demeanour with which he had bullied and dominated the outlaws when he had first re-organized them in the gorge. But it was difficult. He was still a young man, and he looked around now with the open-eyed wonder of a boy as they rode through some cathedral city, down the narrow streets with the houses crowding in upon them, and nearly meeting above their heads. He gaped as did the other men at the towering spire of the cathedral, and the rows of stalls and shops, and the dense crowds of people who swarmed about them.

They were not the only soldiers on the roads that led to Portsmouth. As they reached the top of a hill one morning, and could see the old Roman road stretching out ahead as straight as an arrow shaft across the countryside, they noticed the drifting clouds of dust, and the glitter and sparkle of the sun on helmet and steel that marked another column such as theirs. From every corner of the kingdom, it seemed, armed men were converging upon the coast.

Sir John commanded the company with a quiet assurance. He had laid down certain rules, and he punished severely any offenders. But he was fair, and he was unsparing in his efforts to see that the men were well fed, and that their quarters each night were comfortable. He treated everyone alike, with a pleasant courtesy, and before they had left Grosmont, he had learnt all their names. On the first day of the march one bowman had fallen out to chase a chicken. Before he had run more than a few yards a clear, high-pitched voice from the front of the column had addressed him by name, followed by a description of his appearance and behaviour that brought a roar of laughter from every bowman. But there was little need for punishments. Contented men, as Sir John knew, were easy to handle.

They reached the coast suddenly and dramatically. One moment they were riding slowly up to the crest of a long green ridge that ran across the downs, and then at the summit the trumpeter blew, and the knights and squires shouted and waved their spears.

Hugh leant forward eagerly in his saddle. The road ran over the hill and swept down the green, bare slopes towards a circle of grey walls. Beyond them—and hemmed in tightly, it seemed from that distance—was a tangle of slanting roofs, towers, and spires, and beyond again was the greatest wonder of all, the sea, a tumbling, restless vastness of water as far as the eye could see. Many of the men in the column, Hugh among them, had never seen the sea before, and they pointed and exclaimed, and pointed again to the stumpy little ships with gaily painted sails that were moving across the bay, and the hundreds of others moored in lines by the quays, their masts so thickly clustered together that they reminded the outlaws of the bare trees of the forest in winter time.

The column halted outside the walls of Portsmouth, and the

marshals who had ridden out to meet Sir John led them to an empty piece of ground. Sir John ordered the tents to be pitched and a meal to be cooked. Some of the knights sat down outside their tents, but Sir John, Hugh noticed, walked around the

camp, inspecting the tents, tasting the food, and not until he had seen that every man had eaten did he sit down himself. When he had finished he sent for Hugh.

'Sit you down, Hugh,' he said. 'We shall be here for a week or more. The King is on his way from Windsor. The men may go into the town, but they must be outside the walls again at dusk. The marshals tell me there has been a good deal of trouble, drunkenness, rioting, and looting, and the sheriff and his officers are hanging offenders in future. So warn the bowmen, Hugh. They won't get any sympathy from me if they find themselves in trouble.'

'Yes, my lord,' Hugh said. 'And I will set up some butts for archery practice. That will keep them busy. They're still slow, Jack says.'

Sir John turned to watch another column of men that was just arriving. The knight in the van was in full armour, and on his shield was his coat of arms, a lion's head on a black field. Hugh stood up quickly. It was Sir Henry Mortimer.

Sir Henry was looking about him with his languid, brooding air. He reined in abruptly when he caught sight of the standard with the black hawk. He dismounted, and a squire ran up hastily to hold the horse.

'You will say nothing, Hugh,' Sir John said quietly.

Sir Henry walked towards them, his mail jingling at every step. He bowed stiffly to Sir John, who nodded with an equal curtness, and Hugh remembered a remark that Sir John had once made that he had no love for Sir Henry Mortimer.

Sir Henry's cold blue eyes turned to Hugh, but he showed no sign of recognition.

'Then it is true, Sir John,' he said.

'What is that?'

'That you have recruited a band of outlaws who should have been hanged long ago. Men who broke into my castle of Goodrich, murdered my own men, and carried off two of their friends I was about to hang. And their leader is standing by your side. Did you know that, Sir John?'

'I did.'

'This is an affront to me, Sir John.'

The two men faced each other with a cold disdain. Sir Henry, in his mail and plate, his pale, set face framed in a bascinet, was a head taller than Sir John Carey, and seemed even larger in every way, for Sir John had stripped off his armour at the end of the march, and was wearing a plain jupon and hose. He was a slight and wiry figure now, but he was quite unperturbed, Hugh noticed, and he possessed a natural air of dignity and assurance.

'Well, Sir John?' Sir Henry's voice had risen a note, as if he was irritated by the other's quiet and obvious dislike of him, and his complete unconcern.

'I choose what men I wish,' Sir John said. 'You forget who I am, Sir Henry. I am answerable to no man save the King.'

'Then I shall go to the King when he arrives. But you have made this a personal matter, Sir John. I will meet you tomorrow.' He pulled off one of his steel gauntlets, and threw it on the ground at Sir John's feet.

Sir John smiled and shook his head.

'You will not meet me?' Sir Henry said. For once he showed

a sign of strong emotion, and the blood had come to his face. Hugh stirred uneasily.

'No, I will not meet you,' Sir John said, and he smiled.

The smile infuriated Sir Henry. He took a step forward, and then restrained himself with an effort.

'You have a reputation for courage,' he said. 'Another of these lying rumours.'

Sir John laughed, and he shook his head. His tone was even pleasant and friendly.

'You presume too much, Sir Henry,' he said. 'I do not cross swords with every bully in the King's army. You should know that.'

Sir Henry stepped back, and his hand went to the hilt of his sword. Hugh had never seen such a malignant fury in a man's face before. But Sir Henry stiffened, and his face cleared as if he had wiped it with a cloth. He turned and clanked away. Sir John shrugged his shoulders, and sat down again on the stool outside his tent.

'I am sorry, my lord,' Hugh said. 'It is my doing. He will go to the King.'

'He'll be a fool if he does. I have been very close to the King for many years, and I think Sir Henry will remember that. But keep your men away from his, Hugh, and have a care for yourself. Sir Henry's ways are not pretty ones.'

Hugh explored Portsmouth the next day with Geoffrey and Jack, who said that he had been there before. The streets of the port, narrow enough at any time, were almost impassable now, for they were crammed with the soldiers from every company, men who came from all corners of the kingdom, and many with dialects and accents so broad that Hugh could barely understand a word they said. There were, too, the hundreds of inevitable hangers-on who followed any army; beggars, frauds and quacks, pedlars and acrobats, all anxious to relieve the gullible soldiers of their pay.

In the main square a dense crowd had collected around a platform in the centre, and Jack grunted and butted his way forward.

'A hanging,' he said. 'I haven't seen a good hanging for a couple of years.'

Hugh glanced at Geoffrey, who shook his head. They could be hard and merciless if necessary, and had ordered several hangings in the forest, even the placid and easy-going Geoffrey, but they took no particular pleasure in the death of another man. They pushed their way out of the square and down a side-street which was not so crowded. But a group of bowmen and men-at-arms blocked the way half-way along, and Geoffrey and Hugh, both much taller than the average, saw over the heads of the soldiers a portly fellow in a black robe, who was holding up a sheet of parchment.

'A pardoner,' Geoffrey said with disgust.

They had both seen one before, in Skenfrith, selling pardons for considerable sums of money to superstitious villagers and villeins, and then tempting the people to buy worthless relics.

'I have just returned from the Holy Land,' the pardoner was saying. 'See what I was given in Jerusalem, in the shadow of the Church of the Holy Sepulchre!'

'The fat old fraud's never been outside England,' Geoffrey said. 'What's that he's selling?'

The pardoner was holding up small pieces of cloth.

'I'll bet you a week's pay it's from the sail of St. Peter's fishing-boat,' Geoffrey said.

He was right. The soldiers gasped and pressed forward eagerly to see such a marvel, and they handed over enough money to have bought a small boat. Geoffrey growled angrily, and Hugh dragged him away before he started a riot.

They went down to the quays and the wharves where the ships were being collected from all along the south coast to ferry the army across the Channel. These were greater wonders to Hugh and Geoffrey than any relics the pardoner could have shown them, and they wandered about for several hours, and only started back for the camp as the sun began to set. But though they could have found their way through the trackless forest, they were soon lost in the maze of winding streets.

They stopped in an alley, with decrepit old houses on either side, the upper stories leaning out crazily and dangerously over their heads, and blotting out what little light there was from the sun. It was a dirty, gloomy, and smelly spot, and they walked slowly, hoping to see someone who could direct them to the north gate of the town. But the doors of all the houses were shut, and the alley was silent and deserted.

'Someone coming,' Hugh said.

From behind was the sound of running feet, and two men-at-arms came round the corner.

'There they are!' one of them shouted. They did not pause. They rushed for Hugh and Geoffrey, and as they came they whipped out their swords.

But the forest had trained Hugh and Geoffrey to sudden alarms, and for big men they could move very quickly. They leapt aside, Hugh to the right, Geoffrey to the left. It was not far, but it made their attackers hesitate and turn direction, and it gave them time to draw their own swords. Instinctively Hugh raised his sword, and sidestepped again. A white face in the gloom and an open, shouting mouth glared at him, and a sword swished over his head as he ducked. He heard another shout from his left, and the clash of blades, and then his man was stabbing at him with a yell of triumph. Hugh thrust the blade away, but the man could use a sword. He swung up his weapon with a frightening speed, and hacked down. A brilliant flash of light seemed to blind Hugh, and a tremendous, shattering blow came down on his helmet. He staggered back against the wall of the house, and only his great strength kept him on his feet. He pushed out his own sword, opened his eyes, and jumped forward. If he let himself be pinned against the wall, he would be lost.

He saw the white surcoat, and the unmistakable crest of the lion's head of Sir Henry Mortimer, but there was no time to think about that. He thrust again at the full extent of his long reach. His sword was nearly wrenched from his grip. He felt the blade shudder, and heard a shrill scream, and he stumbled forward, and thrust again, straight for that white surcoat, with the same shock up his wrist, and this time a strangled gasp came from his opponent as he crumpled and fell.

Hugh looked for Geoffrey. He was against the same wall, enormous in the gloom, and growling like a bear that was being baited by a pack of dogs. As Hugh ran to join him, he swept away a cut at his head, and then his man turned and rushed down the alley.

'Run for it!' Hugh said. 'If the sheriff's men stop us we'll hang for fighting in the streets!'

They sheathed their swords, and ran around the corner, not particularly caring which way they went.

'Walk! Walk!' Hugh said urgently. 'Someone coming.'

They strolled past a group of soldiers who had just come out of a tavern, though they would have been too drunk to notice anything suspicious.

'That way!' Geoffrey said. They hurried across the street, and there was the north gate. Two men at arms with spears stood on guard under the archway, but they glanced indifferently at the two men who sauntered past them, two out of hundreds of soldiers returning to their camp outside the walls.

'Hurt, Geoffrey?' Hugh asked.

'No. You killed your man, didn't you? They were Sir Henry's. Did you see their surcoats?'

Hugh nodded. 'They'd been following us. Sir John warned me, so I'd better tell him.'

The flap of Sir John's tent was open, and he was sitting inside with an oil lamp on the table, writing and frowning, for he was not a man of letters.

'What is it, Hugh?'

'Two of Sir Henry's men attacked us in the town, my lord.'

Sir John put down his pen and looked up at the two tall and formidable figures standing in the opening of his tent. He smiled.

'Well, they must have been fools or brave men to tackle you two,' he said. 'Did you kill them both?'

'Only one, my lord. The other ran away.'

'Wise man. Did anyone else see this?'

'No, my lord. It was in a side-street. But they knew who we were. One shouted, "There they are!" when they caught up with us.'

Sir John stroked the tip of his pointed nose with the feather of his pen.

'We'll wait until Sir Henry makes a complaint to the sheriff. But I doubt if he will, I am a better friend of the sheriff than he is. Now listen, Hugh. You must never go out of the camp by yourself. See that someone like Geoffrey or Jack Cherryman is with you. And you had better not say anything to the other foresters. They might start a fight with Sir Henry's men, and that would give him an excuse to make trouble.'

'Yes, my lord,' Hugh said. 'And I am sorry about this.'

Sir John laughed. 'Your men are the best disciplined I have ever led,' he said. 'So you need not worry, Hugh. Perhaps it would be better if I had accepted Sir Henry's challenge and taught him a lesson.'

Hugh looked at Sir John sitting there, and frowned, for the knight, despite his fame as a soldier, seemed a somewhat frail and harmless man compared to the formidable Sir Henry. But Sir John saw the doubtful expression on his face and laughed.

'I have some skill with the sword, Hugh,' he said. 'And with the lance. I was given the Queen's golden cup at the great tournament at Windsor last Christmas.'

'I did not know that,' Hugh said in surprise.

Sir John waved his pen at them in dismissal, and turned again with a sigh to the letter to his wife.

A week passed, of dry, hot weather, and Hugh kept the bowmen busy at the butts. He saw no more of Sir Henry, and apparently no complaint had been made to the sheriff of Portsmouth.

He was lying on the grass outside his tent one afternoon, his head propped against a pile of blankets, watching Nick and Jack trimming feathers. He turned his head as he heard shouts and the sound of running feet. Trumpets were blowing from different parts of the great camp. A fight or a riot, he supposed; the army had been waiting here for a week, and some companies for longer. The men were bored and restive. One of Sir John's pages, young Robert de Camville, a boy of fourteen, rushed past, shouting.

'What is it, Robert?' Hugh asked.

'The King, Hugh, the King! He is riding over the downs!'

Hugh jumped to his feet. He should have stood up slowly, he thought, and sauntered over casually, as befitted a Captain of Bowmen, but he was shedding some of his dignity. Perhaps it was the example of Sir John, who seldom made any pretence of hiding his emotions, and was always natural, friendly, and pleasant.

The road was already lined with knights, men-at-arms and bowmen, all looking towards the downs where dust clouds were drifting over the light-green slopes. The sun flashed on armour, and Hugh could see an apparently endless column flowing down the hill towards the gates of Portsmouth.

Two men came trotting down the road, both in full armour, and shouting to the crowd to keep into the sides. A hundred yards behind rode a solid column of knights, a brilliant stream of black and grey horses, of brightly coloured shields and jupons, the continual shimmer of mail and steel, the tall, slender lances and the tiny pennons, the proud chivalry of England riding to war.

There was a pause after they had passed, and then came another long column of horsemen, archers this time, and at their head Hugh saw the brown, lined face of Giles Allerton. They waved their hands to the crowd, shouting greetings and rude replies to the bellowed jests that cheered them in every accent from the North Country to the borders of Wales.

Then they had passed, and the dust settled slowly. But from the left rose a deep roar of cheers, and Hugh craned forward to look up the road. A single horseman clattered past, carrying a great banner with the sprawling leopards of England emblazoned on the heavy folds, and twenty paces or so behind were two riders.

Neither was in armour; one was in a riding-dress of dark velvet, much older than his companion, and this man, Hugh realized, must be the King, the third Edward, acclaimed already as one of England's most warlike rulers. He was tall and strongly built, riding with the grace and ease of a magnificent horseman. His hair and neatly trimmed beard were dark, and his long face was somewhat olive in colour. He was watching the wildly cheering soldiers who lined the roads, and his cheeks were flushed, and his eyes gleamed with pleasure. He turned his head and spoke to the boy at his side.

'The Prince of Wales,' said a squire standing by Hugh.

The young Edward, despite his youth, was an experienced soldier, and he carried himself with the assurance of a much older man. He was shorter than his father, with broad shoulders, and gave an impression of great strength and endurance. Though he was destined never to sit on the throne of England, he rode now in the warm sunshine and through the ranks of shouting men and waving swords in all the vigour and freshness of his youth, the boy who would become, under the name of the Black Prince, one of the most famous soldiers in Christendom.

The army began to embark the next morning, for a new sense of urgency and speed spread over the port and the camps now that the King had arrived. For the past week the bowmen and spearmen had been employed in filling the holds of the ships with food and supplies, and now they began the slow and exasperating business of leading the thousands of horses on board, and stabling them in the stumpy little ships that lay alongside the quays.

But it was finished at last, though there was little space left by then for the bowmen to sleep on the ship in which Hugh and his men found themselves. Sir John was the last to cross the gang-plank, and he ordered his standard to be hoisted, and his shield hung over the side.

The ship was broad and short, with two high platforms at bow and stern, the fore and maincastles, as Hugh had heard them called, and used as fighting stations by the bowmen, if the fleet was attacked at sea. In the centre was the single mast and its huge sail, and everywhere, to the bewildered eyes of the landsmen, were ropes and tackles, and more ropes again, like the intricate network of a spider's web.

The sailors were barefooted, brown-faced men, who used a language of their own, so Hugh thought, with words and phrases to describe the various parts of the ship and the different ropes that he had never heard before. They greeted the bowmen with grins and lurid jokes about seasickness, and pushed them cheerfully about the ship and out of their way, bellowing orders about backstays, dead-eyes, bunt-lines, forestays, and shrouds.

Hugh leant over the side and watched the busy scene as the fleet put out to sea. Trumpets were sounding incessantly as the sails were hoisted, each with some gaily painted device, while long pennons fluttered from the mast-heads, and over the sides were the painted shields of the knights and squires.

Sir John stood on the maincastle with his trumpeter, in full armour, calm and imperturbable amidst all this bustle and noise. By his side the grey-haired master of the ship leant on the long oar that acted as a rudder, and with a creaking of blocks and pulleys the sail was swung up. The trumpet sounded a long blast of excitement, so it seemed to Hugh, and as he looked down, a sailor close by untied a rope and flung it on to the quay. Already there was a gap of dark-green water between the ship and the wooden wharf.

The deck heaved and pitched, and Hugh clung to a rope. The bows dropped with a sudden and unpleasant lurch, and Hugh gasped as a handful of salt-water splashed across his face and eyes. He saw the coastline and the sand dunes spreading out to right and left, and the grey walls of the town, and behind him as he turned to look, was the bare, shimmering expanse of the sea, and somewhere, over the horizon, was the coastline of France. The little ship rolled and then pitched again; Hugh closed his eyes, and his stomach began to turn. He groaned, and leant over the side, and cursed the day that he had ever left the cool shades of the forest, and the feel of the firm turf beneath his feet.

10

THE STORMING OF CAEN

The coast of Normandy, Hugh thought, as he stood on the forecastle, was a disappointment. In some way, he had felt sure, it would be completely different to that of England. But the line of sand dunes and the gentle slopes of green behind were the same as those he had left at Portsmouth. Even the church tower which he could see, and the huddle of wattle and daub huts, and the fields divided into long strips, were exactly the same as those at Fingle Cross, or any village near the forest.

He had expected, too, to find a huge French army barring the landing of the English. But there was no one. Those knights who were first ashore, and had ridden a few miles inland to scout, reported that there were no French troops in the area.

The march of the army began three days later, with the mounted men, the knights, the men-at-arms, and the bowmen with horses, in one column, and the spearmen and the bowmen on foot, in the other. The line of the march was marked by the black smoke from the burning villages; what the English wanted, they took, and the rest they burned or smashed. Warfare, Hugh soon discovered, was not entirely a business of two armies locked in a desperate battle; it was a dirty, sordid, and brutal affair, too, of loot and murder and destruction. He said something of this to Sir John Carey, outside the knight's tent, by the side of a camp fire at the end of the day's march. With Sir John was one of the other knights of the company, Sir James Valence, who had a small manor at Whitchurch, on the borders of the forest. He was a young man, little older than Hugh, cheerful and penniless, who made no secret of his debts, and his reason for joining the army. Only a large ransom from a great French nobleman would enable him to pay for his new suit of armour, and clear the other debts on his estates. He had at one time quarrelled with Sir Henry Mortimer, had challenged him, and was then beaten to the ground with a smashed collar-bone. He had heard with delight the story of Jack

Cherryman's rescue from Goodrich, and had made up a song about it, for he was a good musician, and was seldom heard, even on the longest and hottest march, without a song on his lips. He treated Hugh with respect and a good deal of friendliness.

Sir John listened to Hugh's complaints about the behaviour of some bowmen from another company whom he had seen that morning burning and ransacking a village, after treating the French villeins with an appalling brutality.

'You must forget your romantic ideas of warfare, Hugh,' Sir John said.

'I never had any, my lord. There was no room for romance in the forest. But my men, outlaws though they were, never behaved like that.'

Sir James chuckled, and refilled his mug with wine.

'I did hear of some outlaws who broke into the castle of a knight of high repute, may he rot in hell, locked him inside his own keep, knocked his sentries on the head, and escaped over the walls with two of his prisoners who no doubt deserved to be hanged.'

'Did they not harm the lord of the castle, James?' Sir John asked.

'No, sir, unfortunately. I mean, of course, that that would have been a dreadful crime.'

'Dreadful,' Sir John said gravely.

Hugh looked from one friendly face to the other a little uncertainly, for he was a serious young man, and unused to this gentle raillery. The task of welding together the outlaws into a stable community had not been an easy one for a person of his age. He had not done it by kindness or gentle persuasion.

'You must unbend, Hugh,' Sir John said.

'How do you mean, sir?'

'You can lead men in several ways. One is by a ferocious discipline. Another is by patience and understanding. I believe in the second. Now, take Sir Henry Mortimer . . .'

'And throw him into the nearest river,' Sir James said fervently. 'And tie a heavy weight around his neck!' He drained his tankard and laughed cheerfully.

Sir John smiled. 'His men obey him from fear.'

'I don't blame them,' Sir James said.

'James, if you would let me finish? But will they do so in the middle of a fight when things go wrong? They are much more likely to drive a shaft through his back.'

'But you must have discipline, my lord,' Hugh said.

'Of course. But my kind, not Sir Henry's. So, unbend, Hugh.'

'I will try, sir.'

'I am sure you will. You are a good leader now, and you will become even more so when you carry a lance and a coat of arms on your shield.'

Hugh sat up with a jerk. 'I, sir? A coat of arms?'

'Why not? Lesser men than you have done so, and risen to knighthood. You will have me to help you.'

'And me,' Sir James said. 'You can help me to pay my debts then.'

Towards the end of June the army encamped near the city of Caen, the most important town they had seen since landing. Sir John said there would be some serious fighting at last, for the French would not surrender such a rich prize tamely.

There had been a succession of heavy summer rainstorms; they had laid the dust on the roads of Normandy, but it was very hot now as the English pitched their tents. Hugh threw down his helmet thankfully, and stripped off his brigandine. He was soaking with sweat, and he longed for the deep pool in the gorge where the outlaws used to swim in the summer.

But he carried little compared to the heavily armoured knights. All, including the squires, wore mail from head to foot, and those who could afford it, had in addition the pieces of steel which were now in fashion. Sir John and Sir James wore demi-vambraces and brassarts of steel over the mail on their arms, roundels to cover the armpits and elbows, and more plates strapped around each leg. Over all that was the jupon with an embroidered coat of arms, and beneath everything a quilted gambeson against the skin as a protection against bruising by a blow on the mail-links. Once in battle, and the front of the bascinet pulled down, they would be grilled by the sun, sweltering and burning with heat. Hugh was glad that he did not have to wear such a load, as he drank a tankard of wine that Jack handed him, looted from a village that morning.

At dawn they moved off again, a short march that ended near the banks of a broad river. Sir John ordered the bowmen to dismount, and formed them up in three lines facing him. They all looked curiously across the river, and at the city of Caen on the farther side. The houses immediately opposite came down to within fifty paces of the bank, and there were no walls or defences at this point, probably, Hugh thought, because the width of the river was considered protection enough against an attack.

To the left was a bridge with a gatehouse on the town side, and the tall double-doors were shut. A dead horse lay in the centre of the bridge, and several bodies of English soldiers were scattered on the bank, and one with his head and shoulders leaning over the parapet.

Sir John had told Hugh one evening that he invariably tried to explain his plans before a battle to all his men. They would fight the better, he said, if they understood what they had to do.

'The River Orne,' he said, pointing to the swirling water, for there was quite a considerable current. 'That is the Old City to the left, as they call it, with the castle on the higher ground against the far walls. The New Town is to the right, and is divided from the Old by the bend in the river. The King has already taken the Old Town. We are to storm the New.'

They looked at the broad river and the dead bodies on the bridge.

'There are cross-bowmen in those houses near the bank,' Sir John said. The helmeted heads were visible at the open windows. 'The Earl of Warwick will cover the bridge with fire from his bowmen. There they go now.'

Wagons were being pulled by hand into position at the end of the bridge as a protection against the cross-bows, and already Hugh could see the short black bolts flying across the river. Two bowmen went down, and the others crouched behind a wagon.

'All the foresters can swim, Hugh?'

'All, my lord.'

'That is what I told the King, and that is why we are here.'

'Can't swim with bows, my lord,' Jack said. 'The water will ruin the strings, and the feathers on the shafts.'

'I know that, Jack Cherryman. Do you think this is the first time I've stormed a town, or led bowmen into action?'

'No, my lord,' Jack grinned.

'You won't need your bows. Leave them here with the wagons. Sword and dagger will do the business. As soon as you start to swim, the Earl's bowmen will loose at the houses. That should make the cross-bowmen keep their heads down. Storm the houses, and then make for the gatehouse. Kill the men there and open the gates. We shall be on the other side with a battering-ram to help you, and I shall be the first across.'

Sir John looked at the brown, resolute faces, and then at Hugh, and his forehead wrinkled in silent inquiry. Hugh nodded.

'Brigandines off,' he said. 'They'll weight us down in the water. Keep your helmets on if you like. I hope those bowmen of the Earl know how to use their weapons, my lord.'

'They do. They're the King's own Bowmen, led by Giles Allerton.'

'I know Giles,' Jack said. 'If he trained those bowmen, we needn't worry.'

'Then I'll meet you in the town,' Sir John said. 'Find me a good billet for the night, Jack.'

Jack spat and grinned. 'Trust me, my lord. It won't be the first time I've stormed a town, either.'

A roar of laughter went round the bowmen, and Sir John's eyes gleamed; these tough foresters were the best men he had ever led into battle. They were ready now, stripped down to shirt and hose, sword and dagger at waist, and waiting for Hugh to move. He walked down to the water; his knees were shaking, and he hoped that the others would not notice. But far worse was the emptiness of his stomach. It was like that dreadful nausea that had swept over him on the boat when they left Portsmouth, but this, he knew, was fear. He turned his head and grinned at the foresters.

'Take it slowly at first,' he said. 'Keep your strength for the other side. Spread out well in the water.'

He waded out; the water was delightfully cool, and he threw himself forward and began to swim with long deliberate strokes. The current was strong, and would push them down-stream a little, so he changed direction to the right.

A trumpet blared from the bank behind. He heard the familiar sound of bowstrings, and a flight of cloth-yard shafts whistled overhead. Something hit the water on his right, and he saw a bolt coming low across the river. It hummed over him; a man screamed, and Hugh increased his speed, thrashing out with arms and legs, trying not to think of those cross-bows on the other side.

His feet touched the bottom. He stumbled forward through the clinging mud that sucked at his feet, and drew his sword and dagger. His fingers were wet and slipped on the hilt, but he was clear of the mud now, and on firm ground. Head down and shoulders hunched, he ran up the slope of the bank, Jack panting hoarsely on his left, and the huge figure of Geoffrey by his side.

The line of houses was twenty paces away now. A last flight of shafts swooped down from behind, clinking against the stone-work or vanishing through the black, gaping windows and doors. Hugh swerved towards the nearest doorway, and as he did so a man appeared in the opening, a cross-bow raised to his shoulders. Hugh stopped and dropped to the ground; the

stumpy bolt whizzed over his helmet. No time to rewind, he thought, as he rushed forward, his wet feet squelching on the ground, his hose chill and clinging on his legs. The cross-bow man had jumped back inside the house, and Hugh burst through the door. The man shouted and raised his bow, and Hugh lunged at him frantically, head down, arm at full stretch. He felt his sword drive home, and then Geoffrey yelled and brought his sword down with a clash and a screech of steel on the fellow's helmet.

Ahead was a narrow passage and another open door, with bright sunlight beyond. Hugh ran down the passage and out into a narrow street. The foresters, yelling and waving swords, appeared at the other doors to the right and left.

'Left!' Hugh yelled. 'Round me! To the gatehouse!'

Geoffrey closed in on one side and Jack on the other, and in a solid group they ran down the street. Men in leather jerkins and with helmets came out of the houses and formed up in a block across the road.

'At them!' Hugh yelled. He was no longer conscious of fear. Instead he was filled with a sense of fighting madness such as he had never experienced before. He flung himself forward, hacking down at the white and brown shrieking faces. His sword clanged on sword and helmet as he cut and stabbed in a fury of desperation, and then they were through, and there was the gatehouse towering above them on the left.

Half a dozen helmeted men, and one in mail and plate with a painted shield over his left arm, poured out of one of the towers. Oh for our bows, Hugh thought. But he dared not hesitate. Any check now would be fatal.

'On, on!' he bellowed. He heard Nick yelping and screeching, and Jack's hoarse shout as they hurled themselves at the Frenchmen. Geoffrey made for the man with the shield, who raised his sword and crouched down. Geoffrey hacked down with all his strength and great height, and then Hugh was guarding himself against another man, who shouted at him in French. But Jack was stabbing at him, and he fell back against the wall of the tower, and dropped his sword.

A thunderous crash came from the tall, wooden doors. The battering-ram, Hugh thought, and he could hear cheering

voices from the other side. Two long bars of iron ran down the doors, and he heaved at one and swung it up. The door crashed open, knocking him back as a horde of English bowmen ran through and past. There was a single exultant trumpet-call, and a huge black horse swept past Hugh, the hooves drumming on the bridge. He caught a glimpse of the black hawk on the shield, and then Sir John was past and had vanished up the street, with twenty more riders behind him. The town was won.

Hugh leant against the wall, and wiped his streaming face. 'All right, Geoffrey?' he said. 'Jack?'

Jack spat and nodded. He was examining the houses on the opposite side of the street, and pointed with his sword to the most imposing, built of stone and with shuttered windows.

'That'll do!' he said. 'First pickings for us!'

He ran across and smashed open the door. Hugh grinned, and sent some of the foresters back over the bridge to bring the wagons and their precious bows. A stream of English bowmen and mounted men-at-arms was pouring through the gatehouse, and spreading out in the town. There was no more the foresters could do, and perhaps Jack was right, Hugh decided. The fighting was over, and the serious business of looting could now begin. The house that Jack had entered was a substantial one, the home of some rich Caen merchant, and the foresters ransacked it methodically, heaping up everything of value in one of the rooms downstairs.

Hugh watched them for a moment, and then went to see if the wagons had arrived. As he stood by the door, a column of bowmen, led by Giles Allerton, marched smartly up the street. He saw the house, and halted his men.

'Clear off!' he said curtly to Hugh. 'This house is requisitioned by the King's Bowmen.'

Hugh drew a deep breath, and clenched his fists.

'The King's Bowmen can jump into the river,' he said. 'Clear off yourself, before I break your neck.'

Giles stiffened as if he had been stabbed with the tip of a dagger. He scowled, and his hand went to his sword-hilt.

'I'm Giles Allerton, Captain of the King's Bowmen,' he said. 'No one in the army talks to me like that. I'll hang your guts outside this house before . . .'

He broke off, his eyes on Geoffrey, who had just come out of the house, sword in hand, and leaning lazily against the wall, gigantic and formidable, in sodden hose and shirt, the sleeves rolled up to show the enormous muscles of his arms. For the first time Giles Allerton noticed the wet clothes.

'You're Sir John Carey's men who swam the river,' he said.

'That's right,' Hugh said. He smiled, though with little friendliness. 'Now march your pimply little kids away, Master Allerton, before they get hurt.'

'Now, see here,' Giles stepped forward, and then his scowling face broke into a wolfish grin of delight. 'Jack! Jack Cherryman!'

Jack ran forward, and the two veterans hugged each other.

'What's this I heard, Giles,' Jack said. 'I'd give my blood for you, old friend, and I've done so before now. But no one takes my loot, and you should know that.' He patted Giles on the back and grinned at him, like a tame bear, Hugh thought, friendly one moment, but liable to tear and rip the next.

'D'ye remember that thieving Kentishman who tried to steal our silver plate after the sack of Falaise?' Jack asked. 'He needed a surgeon by the time we'd finished with him. I give you fair warning, Giles, old friend,' and Jack beamed at Giles, and patted his back again, 'we've ninety good bowmen here from the forest of Goodrich, and we're not afraid of any man in the King's army, let alone the King's perishing bowmen.'

Giles shook his head, and laughed, though he was watching Jack warily. 'I would as soon upset a wasp's nest with my bare hands,' he said. 'Goodrich, eh? Then you're the men who bearded Sir Henry Mortimer in his own castle? Jack, there's no man in the army who would cross your company. And I've seen you before,' he added, looking at Hugh. 'The bowman of Skenfrith. So you're Hugh Fletcher.' He laughed, showing his yellow fangs. 'Well, Master Fletcher, I cry you pardon. And it's not often that Giles Allerton says that. You ask Jack here. Now, you see that tavern down the street? That's our billet. Bring your friends there tonight, Jack, and I'll keep a few barrels of wine back for them.'

He shouted at his men, and they marched away down the street. Jack shook his head and spat with great satisfaction.

'Requisitioned by the King's Bowmen!' he said. 'Giles hasn't changed. And you're learning, Hugh. Anyone who tries to get between you and your loot needs a dagger in his windpipe.'

A dozen horsemen clattered down the street, and when they saw the standard of the black hawk outside the house, they pulled up. It was Sir John and his knights and squires.

'That was well done, Hugh,' he said, 'and I shall tell the King so. This looks a good billet, Jack.' As he went inside, Sir James Valence was lifting a sack from his saddle. It clinked loudly, and he winked at Hugh.

'This should pay some of my debts to Isaac of Gloucester,' he said. 'The finest gold plate I've ever seen in a church.'

It was dusk when Jack, together with Geoffrey and Hugh, went in search of the tavern where the King's Bowmen had billeted themselves. Outside the door was a group of bowmen from another company, trying to push their way inside, and a noisy argument was going on that would soon become a fight, Hugh thought.

'Well, it isn't an ale-house any longer!' a voice roared. 'So go and find somewhere else to drink. This belongs to the King's Bowmen!'

Another voice began to argue, but was interrupted by an angry bellow, a scuffle, the sound of blows, and men wrestling, and a man shot out of the doorway. He hit the cobbles with a thud, and rolled over into the gutter and lay still. A huge figure of a man, hands on hips, was silhouetted against the yellow light of the torches within. His barrel of a chest was heaving with his exertions, and he glared out into the street.

'Any more down-at-heel bowmen want a turn with Will of Cheapside?' he demanded. But the bowmen turned and disappeared into the darkness of the street. The giant saw the foresters, and shook an immense fist at them.

'Another crowd of thirsty perishers!' he said. 'Get out of it! Off, pigs-trotters!'

'Giles Allerton asked us to come,' Geoffrey said in his mild tones.

'That's your story, is it?' Will blocked the doorway, and folded his arms. 'You 'eard, you . . .' He described Geoffrey with a string of expressions that were the filthiest Hugh had ever heard, and the speech of the foresters was not always pretty.

'I'm not lying,' Geoffrey said, and his voice was still calm and persuasive. Jack chuckled. He knew his man. That purring voice was sometimes the signal for an explosion of rage from the placid Geoffrey.

'All right!' Will growled. 'You asked for it, pig's meat! Will of Cheapside knows 'ow to deal with muck like. . .'

He swung his fist. Geoffrey slipped to one side almost daintily for a man of his size. His right fist smacked up against Will's chin, a crisp, true punch that sent the Londoner back inside the door. Geoffrey leapt after him like a tiger, growling and snarling, and Hugh laughed. He had seldom seen Geoffrey lose his temper; the last time he had nearly killed a man.

The two giants vanished inside the tavern door in a series of thuds and crashes, and Hugh and Jack pushed their way in hastily. They found themselves in a large room with tables down the side, and crowded with the bowmen of the King's Company. In the centre, sitting on the floor, was Will of Cheapside, wiping away a smear of blood from his nose, his deep-set eyes smouldering with fury.

The bowmen jumped up as Hugh and Jack burst into the tavern. Out came daggers and swords, and the two foresters, joined by Geoffrey, still growling angrily, backed against the wall, and drew their swords. The torchlight glinted on the broad blades, and there was a pause. Giles Allerton jumped on to a table and waved his arm.

'Hold! Hold!' he shouted. 'No fighting! These are friends of mine. I asked them to join us. These are Sir John's bowmen who swam the river and cleared the bridge for us. That's Hugh Fletcher, the outlaw leader of Goodrich Forest, and the man who beat me at the butts at Skenfrith.'

The daggers disappeared, and the swords were rammed home again. Giles wiped his forehead with relief. He was not afraid of a fight with any man in the army, but he respected the Marshals of the army. They would surround the tavern, and there would be half a dozen men hanging in the square of Caen the next morning. Looting was one thing, and accepted as a normal part of the campagin, but unnecessary bloodletting among valuable bowmen was a crime.

Will clambered to his feet. He picked up a tankard from the nearest table and poured the contents down his throat. He was half drunk already, Hugh thought, watching him warily, and in a dangerous mood.

'These scum from the forest may be friends of yours, Giles,' he said. 'But this fat sow here ain't no friend of mine.' His bloodshot eyes were on Geoffrey. 'I'm going to break his perishing neck for him and feed him to the fish in the river. Let him swim again if he can when I've finished with him.'

The empty tankard sailed across the room with enough force to have cracked Geoffrey's head open. But he had been watching the big Londoner, too, and he ducked. The tankard crashed into the wall behind him.

'Fight!' the King's bowmen yelled, and began to pull the tables back. 'Fair fight! No daggers! At him, Will!'

A grey-haired man plucked at Hugh's sleeve. 'Best tell your friend to go,' he muttered. 'Will's the strongest wrestler in London. I've seen him snap a few limbs and bones before this.'

'That's so,' Giles said. 'Take your man back to his billet, Jack.'

Jack chuckled and spat emphatically on the rush-strewn floor. 'I've a good set of silver plate I found in our billet, Giles,' he said. 'Two silver salvers on our man.'

Giles smiled. 'Two salvers it is, Jack.'

Geoffrey stripped off his brigandine, and rolled up the sleeves of his shirt. The bowmen whistled softly when they saw his bared arms, but Will was too angry, and made reckless by the wine he had drunk, to take any warning. Hugh smiled. He had seen Geoffrey wrestle before, and though Will of Cheapside might be as fine a wrestler as they said, and a man of immense strength, there were rolls of fat around his waist, and he looked slow and clumsy on his feet. By contrast Geoffrey seemed slimmer, hard, and fit, with as long a reach as his opponent, and paced in and out with an easy grace, poised on the balls of his feet.

The two men sprang at each other, long arms out, fumbling for the first vital hold. They heaved and strained in the centre of the room, strong legs braced, grunting and panting with their tremendous exertions. Geoffrey broke loose and jumped to the left. Will turned, but more and more slowly, and then Geoffrey's hands were round his throat. With a thud the two big men fell to the floor, Geoffrey on top, Will's thick legs kicking and writhing as he tried to break loose. The bowmen roared and thumped on the wooden tables with their tankards. Will brought up one brown fist and thumped it down on Geoffrey's back with a sound like a drum being beaten. Geoffrey grunted, and hung on. Will tried again, and tore at Geoffrey's hair, forcing his head back. He kicked out viciously and caught Geoffrey in the stomach.

'Foul!' Jack yelled. 'Foul, Giles!'

Geoffrey let go, and rolled over on the floor, his face twisted with pain. But Will was in no condition to take advantage of his kick. He stood up shakily, hands to his throat, his great chest heaving in an effort to refill his lungs, half throttled by that stranglehold of Geoffrey's. Geoffrey stood up, too, and they glared at each other, and Hugh smiled again. He felt almost sorry for Will of Cheapside, for there was an expression on Geoffrey's face that would have frightened most men.

Will shambled forward, arms out and head down. Geoffrey waited for him, and then brought his knee up. It was a savage and dreadful blow. Will staggered back, one hand to his nose, half dazed.

'Foul!' the King's bowmen yelled. 'Foul! Kill, kill him, Will!'

'Will fouled first,' Jack said angrily. 'You saw, Giles?'

'What of it?' Giles said. 'It's a good fight, Jack.'

But Will was no coward. That knee in his face might have finished most men there, but it had merely increased his fury. He rushed in again, punching wildly, and Geoffrey sidestepped coolly. He swung his left fist into Will's bulging stomach, and the Londoner gasped and came to a halt. Geoffrey flung his arms around him, but Will was a skilled wrestler, and so ponderous that even Geoffrey could not lift him off the ground for a throw. And a throw now would be dangerous, for both men had dropped all ideas of rules or fouls; they would not use a dagger, but they still had feet and fists.

They staggered around the room, each trying for a lock on the other's neck or arm, with the bowmen cheering and stamping on the floor. Geoffrey suddenly freed himself and stepped back. His right arm shot out, but Will ducked, and the punch caught him above the eye, and slashed the skin. He was a fearsome sight now, with blood running from his nose and his eye, but he was not badly hurt, and he was very strong. He was still half drunk, though, and his temper had boiled over to the point of recklessness. He yelled a last insult at Geoffrey, and charged at him with a surprising speed, an enormous, bull-like figure, tall and heavy, arms out, a raging bear, and nearly as powerful.

Geoffrey waited calmly. He took the shock of that charge, and, his arms around Will's waist, pivoted and heaved with a deep grunt. Will sailed across the room; he landed on top of the table by Giles and Jack, slid across the smooth surface, carrying with him all the tankards, and smashed into the wall head first. It was a stupendous crash, and he lay there, eyes shut, stunned, and finished.

Giles had jumped clear of the flying monster, and he scowled down at the unconscious wrestler.

'Two silver salvers it was, Giles,' Jack said.

'You win,' Giles said. He kicked Will in the ribs. 'Wake up, you drunken barrel of wine,' he growled. 'Chuck a bucket of water over him, someone. I'll have that fat off him on the march to the north. He can walk for a few days.'

II

GOBIN AGACE

An August sun glared down on Hugh. He slumped wearily in his saddle as his horse plodded along the straight, unending road. They had marched for the last seven days in a nightmare of heat and dust, of thirst and hunger, and the dust, Hugh had decided, was the worst of all. It hung all day over the columns of men and horses as they moved sluggishly along the French roads, it coated his hands and face, his brigandine and hose and helmet. It left long smears of dried sweat and dirt on his unshaven face, and the perspiration ran continually down his forehead and cheeks until he looked as if he had been weeping. Sometimes he wondered where all that sweat came from, for his whole body was dry and parched; his throat was dry, his lips stiff and sore, and he felt as if he had swallowed nothing but dust for weeks.

The English had reached the River Seine in the middle of August, marching steadily from Normandy after the sack of Caen. The French were gathering at last, and a great army that outnumbered King Edward's by four to one, so the wild rumours whispered, was thundering up the roads from the south and east. To stand and fight against such overwhelming odds was more than the King was prepared to do. He was marching north now, and towards the Channel and the ships that would take him home to England.

But when they reached the Seine, the bridge was down. The King swung inland and towards the east, following the line of the river. But at each town the scene was the same, the broken bridge and a broad, swirling expanse of water that neither horse nor man could hope to swim. At Poissy the bridge had been smashed, and to march any farther was to run into the arms of the French. The massive piers of the bridge were still standing, though, and the King had set his carpenters to work. There had been little need to urge them on, for every man in the army knew how desperate their position was, and they had one driving personal cause, too, for anxiety: the long lines of wagons loaded with their loot. Two days later the army crossed the temporary bridge, and set off again for the north and safety.

The French followed grimly and persistently, intent upon a savage revenge for the sack of Normandy. King Edward hurried towards the River Somme; once across that he would be safe. The march was no longer a leisurely one, and a matter of small skirmishes, with long halts to loot and burn. It was a forced, relentless tramp in unbearable heat over the gently undulating countryside and along the straight roads that the Romans had built. Men and horses were exhausted, and food was scarce. Sir John's company had not eaten a good meal for three days, and their horses were dying fast.

Hugh's mount stumbled, and nearly threw him. Geoffrey caught hold of the bridle, for he was on foot. His own horse had died that morning.

'He won't carry you much farther, Hugh,' he said.

Hugh dismounted, and beckoned to one of the bowmen to mount and take his turn in the saddle. Nick was on Jack's horse, white and drooping; he had eaten unripe apples two days ago, and had been sick ever since.

'Not far to the Somme,' Jack said. His voice, hoarse at any time, was cracked and brittle now, and he had not spat for days, Hugh noticed, and he was looking old and tired.

The column halted, one of the many irritating halts, for those in the centre and rear seldom knew the reason. But it was a welcome one now, and they sat down thankfully by the side of the road, flinging off their helmets, and sipping precious drops of water or wine. Men ahead were shouting, but Hugh could not catch the words.

'It's the Somme,' Geoffrey said. 'Something about a bridge.'

Sir John rode up, and dismounted. 'It's down,' he said. His face was streaming with perspiration, for he was in full armour. His bascinet, mail, and steel were white with dust, and his sharp features seemed even more pointed than usual. But he had remained calm and cheerful, encouraging his men, seeing to the sick, trying to find them food, and talking incessantly to everyone, and Hugh, following such a leader, had done the same.

All heads turned instinctively to the south as if they expected to see the dust clouds rising above King Philip's army. But there was only the empty, rolling countryside, and the hard blue of the sky. The French could not be far away, though, Hugh thought, a day's march, perhaps, so Sir John had said that morning.

Trumpets blew from far ahead, and the men heaved themselves stiffly into the saddles, or put their tired and blistered feet down on the unyielding road. Unshaven, ragged and dirty, white with dust, they stumbled on doggedly, heads down and silent, and once more the dust rose and drifted slowly over the trees and the moorland on either side of the road.

The road swung sharply to the left and the north, and there on the right was the river, the Somme, their last obstacle before reaching the coast. All eyes went to it, and then turned away. The current was running fast, and the water was deep, much too deep for them to cross. The splintered wreck of a wooden bridge hung down from the nearest bank. An hour later they passed another bridge, and that was broken, too.

They halted for the night around the little town of Brismont. The sea was not far distant, but the river here had widened into a broad estuary, quite two thousand paces at least, Hugh estimated, and tidal, though quite impassable even at low tide. As the sun set, and the army looked for billets, and the wagons were brought up and the tents pitched, parties from each company went out in search of food and forage for the horses.

Hugh led twenty of the bowmen down a winding track. Their bows in one hand, a shaft in the other, they walked slowly through the gathering dusk.

'A village,' Geoffrey said.

Hugh held up his hand, and the bowmen spread out in a line on either side of him. He nodded, and went forward, sword in hand. Down below, in a broad hollow, was a small village, one straggling street of huts, and a little church. It seemed deserted which was very likely, Hugh thought. The inhabitants would have fled when they heard of the approach of the English army, and they would have taken with them all their food and valuables. But the bowmen were desperate for food.

'Search every house,' Hugh said. 'Jack, take those on the left.'

Methodically they ransacked every hut, smashing through the flimsy doors. A loud clucking came from one, and Jack emerged, grinning and holding a hen. But that was all they did find, with the exception of some stale bread, and one small sack of grain.

At the end of the street was a larger building, the village tavern probably. As the bowmen came near, the door creaked and began to open. They all halted, and up came the bows.

'Hold!' Hugh said.

A head appeared around the half-open door, long grey hair and a white, wrinkled face. It smiled at them nervously, and an old man, thin and bent, shuffled out into the street. To their intense surprise he spoke to them in English, and with the unmistakeable accent and broad vowels of their part of England.

'It does me good to see English faces again,' he said.

They gaped at him in silence. He smiled and bobbed his head nervously.

'You're English?' Hugh asked.

'That's right. Gobin Agace, at your service, young sir.'

His voice was slurred, and he swayed on his feet so visibly that he put out one dirty hand to the door for support. He is drunk, Hugh thought. He watched him carefully and with distaste, for Gobin Agace, if that was really his name, was an unpleasing looking old man, with his sly, nervous smile, his shifty eyes and expression, and his general attitude of cringing servility.

'What are you doing here?' Hugh demanded suspiciously.

'I live here. Been here for twenty years now.'

'Why?'

Gobin grinned, and he glanced up at Hugh's tall figure with an air of sly secrecy.

'Me and my brother had an argument,' he said. 'Took sanctuary, I did, and then crossed the Channel to France.'

'You mean you murdered your brother,' Geoffrey said.

'Now, that's a hard word, murdered,' Gobin said. 'It wasn't no fault of mine, that . . .'

But Jack, who was listening impatiently, took the old fellow by the collar of his filthy cotehardie, and shook him roughly.

'Any food in this place?' he asked, and shook Gobin again.

'Food! There's nothing left here. The villagers took it all with them. Plenty of wine in the tavern here, though. The first free drink I've ever had from Jacques, the tavernkeeper, since I've lived here.'

They pushed past him and into the tavern, a small, dark, and shabby little place, with an uneven floor of hard-packed earth and covered with dirty rushes. There were several barrels against the wall, and the tap of one was dripping wine. Gobin shuffled hastily across to it, and held out a tankard, but Jack pushed him aside and took the tankard himself. Gobin collapsed on to a bench, and leered at them drunkenly.

The foresters all filled tankards and drank thirstily, while Hugh and Jack searched the place for food. But Gobin was right. There was no food to be found, not even in the cellar. Hugh shrugged his shoulders angrily, and went over to Gobin.

'Do you know the country well around here?' he asked him.

'Old Gobin knows everything, young sir.' Gobin put a skinny and very grimy finger to his red nose, and winked. 'The best wine's in that barrel at the end of the room. I was keeping that to the last. You're a fine-looking young fellow, like me at your age, and . . .'

'Is there a ford across the river near here?'

'Ford! Who wants a ford? I want some of Jacques's best wine, I do. But you can have some, young sir. Just like me, you are.' He stood up and swayed, but Hugh pulled him back with a jerk.

'A ford, you drunken old sot! Is there a ford here?'

''Course there's a ford. Now, give me your tankard, boy, and I'll . . .'

'The devil take the wine!' Hugh said angrily. 'You can drown in it tomorrow if you like! Where's this ford?'

The bowmen had heard the word 'ford' and they gathered around Gobin. Every man in the army knew the vital importance of finding a way across the Somme, and had heard that the King was offering a huge reward for information. Their lives depended upon the chance of crossing in the next day or so.

Hugh heaved Gobin to his feet, and shook him until the old man's head bobbed back and forth like that of a doll. He was frightened now, and his head was fuddled with wine. Hugh pushed him away in disgust, and then Geoffrey picked up a bucket of water and emptied it over his head and face. Gobin reeled back against the wall, spluttering and cursing them with a flow of foul oaths that made Hugh scowl. But the shock had sobered him a little, and Hugh pulled out his dagger. He caught hold of Gobin again, and holding the sharp point of the blade under his chin, gently pricked the skin.

Gobin wriggled and yelped with fear, squinting down in

horror at the blade. The malicious glint in his eyes faded, and once more he became the cringing old villain that he undoubtedly was. Hugh felt no pity for him, a self-confessed murderer, underhand, lying, lazy, and drunken, he decided.

'Now, this ford,' he said. 'You said there was a ford. Where is it? The ford, man, the ford!'

'All this fuss about a ford,' Gobin mumbled. He tried to pull his head back, but Hugh held him firmly, with the point still at his stringy throat.

'Where is it?' Gobin screeched as the dagger moved, and he stared up with bloodshot eyes at the hard, brown face above. There was no pity in the set of that arrogant nose and the strong, jutting chin, and the cold, grey eyes.

'At Blanchetaque,' he mumbled. 'Blanchetaque.'

Hugh pulled the dagger away, and Gobin gulped and shook his head, the water still trickling down from his long, grey hair.

'Where's that? How far? Can you take us there?'

'Four miles? Yes, about that,' Gobin said, watching the dagger. 'Old Gobin knows the place. He'll take you there. You'll see I'm paid something, won't you, young sir?'

'If there is a ford.'

Jack spat with impatient disgust. 'He's drunk, and a liar,' he said. 'He'd say anything for a free drink, Hugh. Throw him out in the road, and let's finish this wine.'

'He's right, Hugh,' Geoffrey said. 'You'll get no help from that old sot.'

'It's worth trying,' Hugh said obstinately. 'We'll take him to Sir John. Come on, all of you. We'll probably have to carry him most of the way.'

'And leave this wine?' Jack said. 'Two fat barrels!'

The bowmen nodded, and Hugh clenched his hands. Was this a time, he wondered, for the quiet discipline and orders of Sir John, or the ruthless and overbearing fury with which he had organized the outlaws? But he did not hesitate.

'Listen, you fools!' he shouted. 'Stay here and drink yourselves insensible, if you want to, and wait for the French to come and cut you up. But I'm going to cross the river with the rest of the army and the wagons with your loot. And if any of you straggle back during the night, I'll see that Sir John deals with you and takes the skin off your backs. And that means you, too, Jack!'

There was silence. Jack gaped at Hugh. He had never been spoken to like that before; there had not been the need. Hugh saw their wavering hesitation, and he drew his sword.

'If the army is caught on this side of the Somme by King Philip, we'll be hacked to pieces, and you know it, you fools. But all you want to do is sit here and fill your guts with wine! Now, get out of here! I'll cut down any man who doesn't move!'

'Come on,' Geoffrey said quietly. 'Hugh's right.'

'Yes, he is,' Jack said. 'Come on, you filthy old sot,' and he dragged Gobin towards the door.

The sun was nearly down, and it was dark by the time they reached Brismont again. Gobin was practically sober by then, but exhausted by the long walk, and he stumbled along, half carried, half pulled by the bowmen. But Sir John was not in the house where he had been billeted for the night. He was with the King, his page told Hugh.

'Then we'll take Gobin to the King,' Hugh said.

'Hugh! You must be crazy!' Geoffrey said. 'Sir John would have listened. But take this drunken old murderer to the King? We'll all be handed over to the Provost Marshal, and we'll be lucky if we get off with a flogging.'

'I'll risk that,' Hugh said doggedly. 'You needn't come.' He marched off into the darkness, still holding old Gobin in a tight grip. Geoffrey shrugged his broad shoulders and, without a word, followed him. As for Jack, he spat with even more force than usual, and stumped after them.

There was no difficulty in finding the King's quarters, for he had set up his household in the small manor-house at the end of the main street, and sentries stood outside the tiny gatehouse, with torches and spears. They barred the entrance as Hugh approached, and Geoffrey grunted in dismay.

'I must see the King,' Hugh said.

One of the sentries laughed. 'Clear off, boy,' he said. 'The Provost Marshal has a quick way of dealing with drunken bowmen.'

But in the torchlight under the archway Hugh caught sight of a familiar face, and he called out:

'Master Allerton! Giles! Here!'

Giles ran out, and held up a spluttering torch. 'Hugh Fletcher! What's this? You should know better than to cause a noise outside the King's lodging.'

'Listen, Giles! This old fellow here lives in a village by the river. He knows of a ford.'

'A ford! That's different! Bring him inside here, and let's have a look at him.'

He led them across a small courtyard, up some steps, and into the passageway between the kitchens and the hall of the manor-house. Several torches were burning there, and by their light Giles inspected Gobin.

'This fellow!' He shook his head. 'We can't take him to the King, Hugh. By the look of that red nose, all he knows about is the inside of a tankard of cheap wine!'

Hugh sighed impatiently. But he could not blame Giles. Old Gobin had collapsed on a bench, completely exhausted, and half asleep. He was a miserable sight now, dirty and decrepit, smelling of wine, as unlikely a looking person to lead an army across a river as anyone could have imagined.

'Give him a drink of wine, Giles,' Hugh said. 'He probably lives on the stuff.'

Giles hesitated. But he was not the first man to be impressed by Hugh's strong personality and dogged determination, and that night Hugh was even for him unusually forceful and domineering. Giles turned and shouted to one of the servants from the King's household, and the man hurried up with a tankard filled with red wine. Hugh took it, and held it under Gobin's mottled nose. A shaking hand came up, as if by instinct and long force of habit; the skinny throat gulped, and the wine went down without a pause for breath. The effect was astonishing, like pouring water on a dry and withered plant. Gobin's back straightened, his glazed eyes began to gleam with life, and he looked about him with a show of interest.

'Looking for another drink,' Giles said, grinning. 'He's had enough, Hugh. But you're right. That's his food, the old sot.'

'The money,' Gobin said to Hugh. 'You promised me a reward.'

'When we see the ford,' Hugh said.

'What's this, Giles?'

They all turned quickly at the sound of that brisk, commanding voice. A tall, brown-haired man in a richly embroidered jupon had just come out of the hall, and Hugh recognized him, and bowed. It was the Earl of Northampton, a close friend of Sir John Carey, who commanded one of the wings of the army, and it was he who had planned with Sir John the storming of Caen.

'It's the captain of Sir John Carey's bowmen, my lord,' Giles said. 'Master Hugh Fletcher.'

'Yes, Sir John has spoken to me about him. I saw you swim the river at Caen, Master Fletcher. It was well done. Are you looking for Sir John? He is with the King.'

'My lord!' Hugh said, and the urgency in his voice made the Earl look at him curiously. 'This man here lives in a village by the river. He knows of a ford.'

'A ford!' The Earl swung round to stare at Gobin, and then he frowned. Everyone frowned when they saw Gobin, Hugh thought. 'This old fellow?'

'Yes, my lord. I know he looks what he is, a drunken old man, but I'm sure he's telling the truth. He's sober enough now. The ford's at a place called Blanchetaque, about four miles from here. It's worth trying, my lord. There's no other choice.'

'No, there's not,' the Earl said, but he was more interested in Hugh now rather than Gobin. He was an intelligent man and a good soldier, and there was little need to tell him how desperate was the situation. This unusual Captain of Bowmen was right, the Earl was thinking, and he remembered what John Carey had told him about the man.

'Bring him in here,' he said curtly. 'Master Fletcher, follow me.'

He went through the wooden screens into the hall, filled now with the King's household, knights and squires, clerks, officials, stewards, and servants of all kinds, and the bowmen and men-at-arms of his own Company. They were sitting over the remnants of what had not been a very large meal, Hugh thought; there could not be many in the army who had eaten really well that evening.

The Earl walked down the full length of the hall, and across the dais where the servants were clearing away the plates from the table, and stopped by a door in the corner. Two guards in the royal livery stood there, and they bowed and moved to one side when they saw the Earl. He gestured to Hugh, who drew a deep breath, and followed him through the door.

The room in which he found himself, was long and wide, with a low roof. It was brightly lighted, almost dazzling after the gloom of the courtyard and the dark hall, and it was warm and stuffy, for there was a fire of logs smouldering at the far end. There were two chairs on either side; the King was in one, and the young Prince of Wales in the other. Standing in a semi-circle around them were the commanders of the army.

The King, dark and sombre in his favourite black velvet, was staring moodily at the burning logs; his long white fingers were playing with the golden chain that hung from his neck, swinging it slowly from side to side, and he was paying little attention to the argument that was going on between the other men there. He glanced up as the Earl approached and bowed.

'What is it, William?' he asked.

'The captain of Sir John Carey's bowmen is here, Your Grace.'

Sir John Carey stepped forward, and looked anxiously at Hugh.

'Not in trouble, I hope,' he said quickly. 'It was he who led the bowmen across the Orne, Your Grace.'

'Yes, I remember, John. You spoke to me of him. I wish he could find me as easy a way across the Somme.'

'He might, Your Grace,' the Earl said. 'He's found a man who knows of a ford not far from here.'

Every head turned abruptly, and a dozen pairs of keen eyes inspected the drooping, shabby figure of Gobin Agace. The King sat up with a jerk, and leant forward, his olive cheeks flushed with sudden hope.

'Where is this ford?' he asked.

Gobin started to explain, but he mumbled and stammered, and the King cut him short with an impatient wave of his hand.

'I can't understand a word he says.' He turned to Hugh. 'Your name?'

'Hugh Fletcher, Your Grace.'

'What has this man told you, Master Fletcher?'

'The ford is called Blanchetaque, Your Grace. Four miles, he says, along the road that follows the river to the east. But he may be wrong about the distance, Your Grace.' The King nodded, his dark eyes on Hugh. 'I think he is telling the truth. The ford is a causeway of chalk, and is uncovered at low tide. Blanchetaque would mean the White Ford, Your Grace, and I don't think he has enough sense to make up that sort of story. It all fits, Your Grace. Low tide is at noon to morrow, he thinks, but he is not certain of that.'

'That would be right,' Sir John said in his quiet, confident voice. 'I asked a French peasant yesterday about the tides.'

The King nodded again, but was still watching Hugh.

'The causeway is wide enough for a dozen men abreast, Your Grace,' Hugh went on. 'The wagons could cross too, he said. I asked him that particularly. The local people use it for their farm carts.'

'Anything more?' the King asked.

'No, Your Grace.'

'Well, you have told me more than I could have expected,' the King said. 'You are an intelligent young man, Master

Fletcher, and you have not been afraid to bring this man to me. If he is telling a lie, you will not be to blame. If what he told you is true, then we shall all be greatly in your debt.'

The King sat back in his chair. He examined Gobin once more, and then his eyes went to the fire, and silence fell on the room. It was now for him to make the decision. He sat quietly and relaxed, and the gold chain began to swing slowly.

His commanders, experienced and skilful soldiers, knew some of what was passing through his mind. The position seemed hopeless; his small army, exhausted and half starved, was pinned against an impassable river, with a huge French army that outnumbered his forces by probably four or five to one, advancing rapidly to destroy him. The choice he had to make now was a frightening one, but whether he took advice or not, the final decision could be made by him alone.

If he gave up all hope of crossing the River Somme, then he must fight it out where he stood, for there would be no chance of retreat. But if he believed the story of a drunken and disreputable man, and the confidence of a young Captain of Bowmen, he must march his army to the ford—if there was one at all—across the line of advance of a great French army, his flanks exposed on ground not of his choosing, with no room to manœuvre, and hemmed in against the immoveable obstacle of a broad river.

The English would be like a mouse that has crept unwisely out of his secure hole to crawl slowly across a wide and open space, while two gigantic cats watch him with a merciless patience, waiting until he has reached a point where he cannot retreat or advance to safety once they jump. And jump they will, to pounce and tear him to pieces.

If the ford did not exist, the English would be lost for certain. If it did, they might be caught half on one side of the river, half on the other. Or they could scuttle across before the French pounced.

The risks were appalling, the stakes tremendous. Sir John Carey and all the other noblemen in the room had their estates to lose, perhaps, if they fell prisoner to the French, and were forced to ransom themselves. But the King could lose a kingdom.

He was a Plantagenet, the King of England. His father had left decisions to others, and his throne had fallen about him, and he had gone to a dreadful death. But this Edward was prepared to make his own decisions.

The gold chain came to rest, and the waiting men stirred. The King had made up his mind.

'Sir John,' he said, and his voice was calm and steady. 'You will march out of the town an hour before dawn, with all your company. Take this man with you. If there is a ford, I will pay him a hundred crowns. If there is not one, you know how to deal with him. Seize the ford, cross it, and hold the ground beyond. I will be close behind you with the main body of the army.'

He stood up, a tall, majestic figure, for he looked what he was, a King of a proud country, and his eyes were gleaming. 'Gentlemen, to bed,' he said. 'We have much to do tomorrow. By the Splendour of God, we shall yet show our French cousins with what courage we can uphold the banners of England!'

12

THE FORD OF BLANCHETAQUE

It was still dark when they rode out of Brismont. As they took the narrow, winding road that ran alongside the River Somme, a mist covered the ground, though Hugh could see the tops of the trees that lined the bank. Gobin Agace rode by his side, a tired and frightened old man. He had been promised the hundred crowns the King had mentioned, if he led the English army to the ford. Sir John had assured him of a rope and a tree if he failed. Hugh was wondering now, as he shivered in the chilly damp morning, if Sir John would keep his word, for he was not a brutal man.

Sir John Carey rode on Hugh's right, his bascinet and mail streaming with moisture from the mist. Behind were the knights and men-at-arms of the company, and then the bowmen and their precious wagons. All the men, including those whose horses had died on the march from the Seine, were mounted again, at the express orders of the King.

The Earl of Northampton, who had shared several campaigns with Sir John, and who thought alike on the ordering of a battle, led the rest of the vanguard, with a hundred knights and men-at-arms, and a thousand bowmen. The main body of the army and the rest of the transport were already preparing to march on the same road. The King was no believer in half measures, and he was throwing all his counters on the table now.

Gobin nudged Hugh, and sniffed loudly. 'The ford is close, sir,' he said. 'At least, I think so.'

'I hope so, for your sake,' Hugh said. And for mine, he was thinking. This ambitious plan, with all its risks of complete disaster, was in a sense his doing.

'I can't see anything for this damnable mist,' Sir John said. 'How do you know the ford is close to us, man?'

'The break in the trees, my lord,' Gobin mumbled nervously. His imagination was flitting rapidly from visions of rows of wine barrels which he could buy with his hundred crowns, to a grim picture of a rope and a noose at the end.

Sir John held up his hand. The column halted without further orders, for it had been agreed beforehand that trumpets would not be blown in case there were French troops on their side of the river.

'Let's see,' Sir John said. 'Bring Agace with you, Hugh.'

They trotted off the road and reined in by the water. Gobin cried out in his shrill, cracked voice and pointed eagerly:

'The huts, my lord! See, those huts there!'

Twenty paces to their right were two huts, and between them ran a track branching off from the road, and ending at the river-bank. Hugh peered through the grey dawn and the wet mist, and he thought he could distinguish the dark shapes of two similar huts on the other side of the river, a sure indication that this was indeed a ford.

'Fires!' Sir John exclaimed, and smacked his gauntleted hand on his thigh with a crisp crack of triumph. 'Camp fires!'

On each side of the huts over there Hugh saw small flickering lights; they stretched along the banks for a couple of hundred paces. Sir John laughed, and clapped Hugh on the back, and as he did so two horsemen rode up to them. One was the Earl of Northampton, and the other the King himself, conspicuous by the thin gold crown that encircled the top of his bascinet, and the Lions of England across the front of his jupon.

'Is this indeed the ford, John?' he asked, and Hugh heard the note of anxiety in his voice.

'It must be, Your Grace. There are French camp fires over there. Why else would they be there if there was no ford? And those huts opposite each other, and the track down into the water?'

'You are right, John.' The King stamped his mailed feet on the ground, for they were all chilled with the waiting and the tension of the moment.

'The mist is lifting,' the Earl said. 'And there's the sun.' He pointed to the grey sky, but Hugh shook his head. Even here, hundreds of miles from the forest of Goodrich, his instinct and training told him the points of the compass.

'That is to the south, my lord,' he said. 'The sun will rise there,' and he pointed.

'What's that glow in the sky, then?' the Earl asked.

'The boy's right,' the King said. 'And you should know what that light is, William. Those are camp fires, thousands of them, King Philip's camp fires!'

They stared uneasily at that ominous sight, a flickering, reddish glare that stretched across the horizon, and then, with one accord, they turned their backs on it, and looked down at the brown water that swirled beneath them. The mist was shredding away, floating in wisps of white and grey on the water, a broad, impassable barrier still to the coast and safety.

Hugh pulled up a tuft of grass and threw it into the water. For a moment it floated motionless, and then it began to move, and drifted away quickly to their left and the mouth of the river.

'On the ebb,' Sir John said.

From the King came a long sigh of relief. His helmeted head turned to the south and that menacing glare in the sky, and Hugh saw his face in profile, the mouth set and the strong chin firm and resolute. The pack might be closing in on him, but he would fight it out to the last.

'Now, John,' he said briskly, 'I will leave the ordering of this to you and William. What have you in mind?'

Sir John did not hesitate. He had not earned a reputation as a soldier of great skill for nothing, and obviously he had made his plans as they rode from Brismont that morning.

'As soon as the river is shallow enough for a man to walk with the water no higher than his knees, I will send Hugh Fletcher here across with his own bowmen. I know of none in the army who can loose so fast and true as they can. I would have William, if he will agree, Your Grace, to post his thousand bowmen along the banks on this side. The range is long, but there will be cross-bowmen over there if I know the French, and cloth-yard shafts at a full cast will spoil their aim.'

'And then, John?'

'When the bowmen are in the middle of the river, they can loose, and then I will lead the van across myself, with all the knights and men-at-arms we have here. After that, it will depend upon our swords and lances.'

The King clapped his gauntleted hands. 'Good, John, good! You agree, William?'

The Earl laughed. 'I always agree with John, Your Grace. It is a good, simple plan, and that is what we need today. Speed and force at the right point.'

'Then that is settled,' the King said. 'And I will see to the crossing of the main body and the wagons. We must get those over. The army would mutiny if we left the loot behind!'

'The cloth-yard shafts are more important, Your Grace,' Sir John said quietly.

'They are indeed, John. They will be the first to cross.' The King raised his hand, and a squire brought up his horse. 'As for Master Fletcher, I am much in his debt. See that you bring him to me later, John.'

There was nothing to be done now, except wait, and that was not an easy matter, so Hugh discovered. He made the bowmen wax their strings, but not brace their bows, for fear of the damp morning, until he gave the word. Few of the men had slept much during the night, for they had made an early start from their billets, and they lay down now, and dozed. As for Hugh, he sat and watched the water. He felt a tremendous weight of responsibility on his shoulders, though his worst fears had gone. They had, at least, found the ford, but they had still to cross. He wanted to pace up and down the banks, and see to the ordering of those other bowmen of the Earl's, but he knew that their captains were experienced and master bowmen, and knew their trade as well if not better than he did.

The current was running fast now, and a broad, white streak was beginning to creep from the end of the track across the river. The last of the mist had gone, and the sun had risen in a clear sky. It would be a hot, fine day. Hugh could see the opposite bank quite clearly at last, and there were the French. Along the bank, on either side of the causeway, were lines of helmeted men, cross-bowmen almost certainly, and drawn up behind was a solid mass of mounted men. The bright morning sun glittered on their bascinets and plate, and even at that distance Hugh could distinguish the gaily-painted shields, the coats of arms on jupons and surcoats, and the many standards and pennons. This would be no leisurely crossing, but a bitterly contested battle, for the French would be as much aware of the importance of the ford as the English. And Hugh realized, too, that casualties among those forcing the crossing would be of little account today. The army must cross at all cost.

Sir John came and sat beside him, his sharp, intelligent face peeping out from his bascinet.

'That old fellow was right, Hugh,' he said. 'You can march twelve abreast across the causeway.'

'Gobin!' Hugh had forgotten about the old man. 'Where is he, my lord?'

'Gone, and with a bag of golden crowns. He'll drink himself insensible tonight.'

'He had better spend the money while he can,' Hugh said. 'If the people of his village know how he earned it, he won't live long.'

'They'll learn soon enough,' Sir John said. 'How else could he lay hands on so much money? Anyway, that is his concern.'

'We shall have to start soon, my lord,' Hugh said. 'Gobin told me that the causeway will not be open for many hours. It will soon be covered again.'

'That is what I had feared, Hugh. Now, when you reach the centre of the river, those French men-at-arms will charge you. Aim for the horses. But I need not tell you that.' Sir John looked at Hugh, for much would depend upon this young man. But there was no fear on that strong face, and Sir John nodded.

'We can stop them, my lord,' Hugh said confidently. 'With horses they cannot cross with more than eight or nine abreast, and they won't be able to open up to outflank us. They will never reach us. The only danger is from those cross-bows.'

'We have a thousand good long-bows on this side. You can trust them, Hugh. As soon as those knights charge you, and you have loosed and halted them, I will bring our knights across. When you see me come, clear a path for us to pass through. Then cross when you can to the other bank, form up on my flank, and loose at anyone in sight. The Earl will send over two hundred more bowmen as soon as you have reached the other side.'

Hugh nodded. His eyes were on the water. 'Not long now, my lord. Jack! See that the bows are braced, and fall the bowmen up, twelve abreast, you and Geoffrey on each side of me.'

He jumped to his feet, and braced his great bow. He ran his fingers over the shafts in his quiver to see that they were loose and he could pull them out quickly, put on his helmet, and drew a deep breath. The crossing of the Orne would be a skirmish compared to this fight. Instinctively he turned towards the south, but the gentle slopes that stretched away towards the horizon were bare and peaceful, shimmering in a haze of heat under the hot sun. But the French must be marching north; they could not be far away. Sir John smiled at Hugh and clanked away to find his horse, and his squire rode up, holding the banner of the black hawk.

'Ready, Jack?' Hugh asked.

The foresters were in column, each man with a shaft already drawn, and ready to nock. Hugh stepped forward and into the water. Ahead lay the broad white strip, still covered with water, but shallow enough to wade through. Hugh looked back and raised his hand, and Sir John did the same.

'Don't loose until I give the word,' Hugh said.

He drew out a shaft, and holding it in his right hand, walked steadily through the water. It was cold on his feet, and then on his hose, but he did not hesitate. A trumpet sounded from the French side, and he heard the cheers and saw the horsemen begin to move down towards the causeway. His hand closed tightly on his bow; by his side Jack was clearing his throat noisily; Geoffrey's face was calm and placid. The water was up to their knees now, and their pace became slower as they splashed doggedly on, the water sparkling and glittering on either side. Never, Hugh realized, had he felt so exposed or lonely, or in such great danger, wading out into the centre of that broad river, with a thousand cross-bows trained on him, and several hundred heavily armoured horsemen waiting to ride him down.

Behind, standing under the great standard of England, the King was watching intently. He, too, knew the sense of loneliness, as did no other man in his army, the weight of responsibility, the crushing burden of doubts and fears. He raised his hand sharply. His trumpeter blew, a long defiant blast, and all the trumpets of the army blew too, a blare of raucous, nerve-tingling fury that stirred the blood of every man in the army. Then the trumpets fell silent, and a deep voice was heard, shouting:

'St. George! St. George for England! St. George!'

All down the road and along the banks the English took up the cry, and their deep-toned cheers of defiance rolled across the river. Hugh laughed; his head and shoulders went back, and the tension vanished. He knew now that he was not alone. There were fifteen thousand men behind him, urging him on, ready to charge and batter those Frenchmen on the other side of the river.

Another trumpet sounded from the English ranks. Hugh heard the twang of hundreds of strings, and then the familiar, heartening whistle of the shafts as they swooped over his head. He followed their flight, and from the lines of cross-bowmen he saw the stumpy, black bolts fly out and across the water, converging on him and the foresters. He clenched his hands and shut his eyes. The bolts screeched over his head. There were screams and the splash of a body falling into the river, and Hugh looked across towards the French. The bolts seemed to move very slowly at first, and then at the last moment they leapt with a terrifying speed, every one apparently coming straight at him. But no one was hit in the front rank, and after the first two volleys, the fire fell off almost completely. For by now the cloth-yard shafts were falling continuously on the cross-bowmen as the Earl's men found their range.

Hugh heard the trumpets sound from the French centre. The knights were trotting down towards the causeway, and then out through the water, their horses throwing up sheets of white spray.

'Stand!' Hugh roared. 'Nock! Aim for the horses!' He waited for a few seconds, eyes on the French. 'Draw and loose! Draw and loose!'

He did not draw himself, though he had intended doing so. But he was so absorbed in watching the French charge and the effects of the long-bow fire that he was hardly conscious of the great bow in his hand. He saw Jack and Geoffrey on either side of him, knee-deep in the water, drawing back full to the ear, and the shafts leaping away.

'Front rank, kneel!' Hugh yelled. 'Second rank, loose!'

He knelt, too, and the strings twanged above his head, and the shafts shot out, the flight flat and true at that short range, plunging at a murderous speed and force into the tightly packed mass of horses. The charge had come to a standstill in a confusion of rearing, wounded, and badly frightened horses. Two turned, and in trying to escape from the shafts that tortured them, galloped off the causeway and into the deep water. Through the white spray Hugh saw a helmeted head appear above the racing water, and a pair of mailed arms, and then they had gone, dragging down their owner with their weight. Then another horse followed, and a third volley of shafts from the foresters hurtled into the shouting, helpless mob, and the chaos was complete. How many French knights were drowned Hugh never knew, for the scene was nearly hidden by the spray thrown up by the horses, and the whole incident was over quickly.

A trumpet was blowing insistently from behind, and when Hugh turned to see the cause he saw Sir John Carey splashing through the water, and behind him a solid mass of English knights.

'Clear the way!' Hugh shouted. 'Clear the causeway!'

As they crowded to either side, the knights began to quicken their pace. Hugh saw the lances go down and the riders crouching low behind their shields; the mail and steel covered figure of Sir John raced past with a shower of spray that drenched Hugh, and hurled itself deep into the raging confusion beyond.

For several minutes the bowmen could do nothing but watch, for fear of hitting their own men. But the impetus of their charge on the already disorganized column of the French was decisive; back went the shouting, slashing mob, and the standard of the black hawk was not far now from the French bank of the river.

The trumpeters of the Earl sounded again, and a second wave of knights galloped across the causeway. Hugh jumped hastily aside as a horse nearly knocked him into the river. He grabbed the stirrup, and was dragged forward violently, half blinded by the spray that shot up around him. In his ears was the clatter and screech of swords, the neighing of horses, the muffled shouts and cheers of men fighting for their lives, the low whistle of the cloth-yard shafts, the high-pitched blare of trumpets, all merging together into a discordant and confused roar of fury and violence.

Hugh let go of the stirrup, and stumbled up the causeway. The knight who had carried him across kicked his horse into a gallop as he reached the level ground, and drove straight into a Frenchman. The lances smashed and splintered against the shields, and both men swayed back under the shock of the impact. But the high saddles held them in place, and they drew swords, slashing away at each other, circling round and round, shouting incoherently, in a frenzy of hot-blooded madness.

Hugh waved and shouted as the foresters came running up towards him. He formed them in two lines and on the flank of the mêlée between the French and English knights. But there were still cross-bowmen on the bank, and Hugh shouted and pointed.

Fifty shafts swept over the cross-bowmen, and then another fifty, and they had gone, stretched out in their line alongside the river. Hugh suddenly realized that he had loosed only one shaft all this time, so engrossed had he been in leading and directing the fire of the others.

'Hold!' he cried, and held up his bow. How many shafts had

they loosed, he wondered? They would not receive any new supply until the wagons crossed; if they did cross, Hugh thought. If they did not, the bowmen would be crippled, useless, and at the mercy of the French knights.

Sir John Carey was reforming his men for a final charge. He had driven the French well back from the river, but a fresh group swung in from the right and against his flank. Hugh shouted and swung round the bowmen. They saw their target, and there was no need to give any orders, but Hugh did so, all the same, and this time he brought up his own bow.

'Loose!' he was shouting. 'Loose!'

There could not have been more than twenty riders in that charge, and fifty shafts were hurled at them as they galloped across the front of the bowmen. Many horses went down; those only wounded swerved away and many horsemen were thrown. Those who were not pinned down by the horses, tried to struggle to their feet, and then the second wave of shafts hit them, mowing them down as the smooth war-heads drove through mail and plate as if they had been paper.

One rider escaped, shielded from the worst of the fire by the other horses, and possibly because he was very heavily armoured with many plates of steel. His lance smashed into the shield of an English knight, and sent him flying from his saddle. He fell with a clang and rolled over, one hand fumbling at his bascinet, and Hugh guessed that the eyepieces had moved and the knight was blinded for the moment. The man pulled up the visor, and managed to get to his knees.

The Frenchman wrenched his horse round and down came the long lance, with the steel-tip and the tiny pennon aimed straight for the kneeling knight, the rider low in his saddle, and only the top of his bascinet showing above the painted shield. The hooves of his horse drummed on the hard ground as he galloped ahead.

Hugh ran forward, nocking a shaft. The Englishman turned and saw the huge black horse thundering down upon him, and above the shield the blank, impassive face of steel, with the menacing, animal-like snout of the bascinet. Hugh halted and loosed at point-blank range, aiming for the throat. The shaft hit the mail gorget with a frightful velocity; it ripped through

the steel links and the thick leather beneath without the slightest check. The Frenchman swayed back under the terrific shock of the blow; he dropped lance and shield and fell sideways from the saddle. One foot caught in the stirrup and his horse swerved and pulled with a jerk.

Hugh caught the reins, and the horse, oblivious of what had happened to his rider, put down his head and sniffed delicately at Hugh.

'You had best take the horse,' Hugh said, turning to the English knight. He gasped and stared, for he was looking down at the long, pale face of Sir Henry Mortimer.

Sir Henry had recognized him at the same moment. His eyes flashed for a second, and then went blank. He stood up slowly, watching Hugh.

'You killed another of my men in Portsmouth,' he said, his voice even and quiet.

'You set them on me,' Hugh said. 'What should I have done, my lord? Stood still and turned the other cheek to them?'

Sir Henry considered him, and then to Hugh's intense surprise he smiled briefly, though it was impossible to tell what particular emotion it displayed.

'I shall deal with you myself next time,' Sir Henry said. He put his foot into the stirrup of the French horse, but a man in full armour could seldom mount unaided, and it was obvious that his fall had shaken and bruised him badly. Hugh bent down, caught hold of his mailed foot, and heaved him up into the high saddle. Sir Henry looked down, and there was no doubt this time about the expression on his face. It was one of puzzlement. He shrugged his shoulders slightly, and gestured towards the body of the French knight.

'My thanks for that, Master Fletcher,' he said. 'I do not cross swords with a bowman and an outlaw, so our scores are equal now.'

'As you wish, my lord,' Hugh said.

Sir Henry nodded, pulled down the front of his bascinet, and rode away. Hugh smiled, and pulled another shaft from his quiver. But the fight was over. The French had ridden away, leaving behind them the dead cross-bowmen in long lines by the river bank, and the main body of King Edward's army was pouring across the causeway. The marshals shouted and waved their arms, for there was no time to be lost. The mounted men galloped through the water, and the footmen ran, and for an hour there was no pause in the stream of men. At last only the wagons remained on the other side, drawn up along the road from Brismont.

The drivers cracked their whips and shouted. The high wheels bumped and splashed through the water, three wagons abreast, and the tide was still on the ebb, and the causeway nearly dry.

Sir John and the Earl stood by the bank, for they were to cover the rearguard now. The King and the knights of his household rode past and up the straight road that led to the north, and only half a dozen wagons were still waiting their turn to cross. Sir John pointed suddenly. Up on the skyline some horsemen had appeared, black dots in the distance, but

the sun flashed briefly on helmet and armour. Then a whole line flooded over the crest, and behind were dark masses of riders. The English trumpets pealed out a warning as the Earl signalled, and the bowmen ran forward to line the bank of the river.

'My church plate from Caen!' Sir James Valence said in anguish. 'Pray God that it has crossed!'

'Our wagons crossed an hour ago, my lord,' Hugh said.

Sir James crossed himself devoutly. 'Then indeed God has been kind to me today,' he muttered. Sir John put his hand to his mouth, and Hugh grinned openly. For the same thought had come to both of them; the clergy of Caen, bemoaning the loss of their plate, would hardly have agreed with Sir James's pious expression of thanks. They would have excommunicated him without any hesitation.

The French vanguard had seen the English, and they galloped furiously towards the river. The last of the wagons came bouncing and splashing over the causeway, and the water was half-way up the wheels, Hugh noticed. The tide was running fast, and the ford would be impassable in a matter of minutes. He nocked a shaft and waited, and on either side of him were the long, waiting lines of bowmen.

From the right another column of French horsemen came charging up the road from Brismont, and the two parties broke into a wild race for the causeway, waving lances and cheering. The first men dashed into the river, and forced their unwilling horses through the rising water. The Earl of Northampton and Sir John exchanged glances, and the Earl raised his hand. His trumpeter blew, and up came a thousand bows.

The air was filled suddenly with the thin shafts, black against the hard blue of the sky, and the deadly hail fell on the French horses crowding into a confused mass near the end of the causeway. Those already in the water reared frantically and fell into the deep river on either side of the causeway, and for their riders there was no hope, for their armour dragged them down below the brown, swirling water. On the bank the confusion became a dreadful chaos of dead and wounded horses, of men trying to gallop out of range of the shafts, and others still determined to cross. On that shouting mob fell another thousand shafts, swooping down slowly it seemed to those watching from the English ranks, but the sharp war-heads plunged down at the last with a fearful speed, on horse and man.

The French vanguard was a shambles. Hugh saw many horses that were maddened with their wounds jump over the steep bank into the river, the spray shooting high up into the air. Most galloped away, carrying with them those who were still trying to advance, and the Earl raised his hand again. As the trumpets sounded the English waved their bows and cheered derisively; they turned and fell in to begin their march to the north. The white causeway had vanished again beneath the tide, and the ford of Blanchetaque was closed once more. King Edward could march to the coast now, and not a single Frenchman would be able to follow for twelve hours.

13

THE CAMP AT CRÉCY

Hugh sat by a camp fire munching a green apple, and hoping that it would not make him ill. He had eaten little that day, but the King had sent out many foraging parties at the end of the day's march, and so every man in the army had had something.

Near him were the tents of Sir John's company, and Sir John himself was sitting on a stool watching the pages cleaning his armour.

'There's still a rust mark on the side of that bascinet, Robert,' he said. 'Use the pumice-stone, boy.'

'Yes, my lord.' Young Robert de Camville began to rub, his serious face intent on his work. Rust was the worst enemy of mail and plate, far more dangerous than any sword or mace blow. Another page was shaking the vambraces and brassarts in a bag filled with sand which was well soaked in vinegar, though a piece of pumice-stone was the last resort for bad rust stains.

The English army was encamped on a low ridge near the little town of Crécy. It was a strong, defensive position with each flank covered by woods, and already the news had spread around the camp that the King had decided to stand and fight.

The situation was no longer a desperate one. A line of retreat lay open to the sea, though it was certain that the French army would outnumber the English, whose strength was now no more than about fifteen thousand. But the French were an undisciplined horde of feudal knights and lords, while the English were veterans, a compact and tightly organized force.

King Edward and his senior commanders knew now, after their experiences at Caen and Blanchetaque, and from previous campaigns in France, that they possessed one supreme advantage, the long-bow. There were over seven thousand skilled bowmen on the ridge of Crécy. They could hurl twenty thousand shafts in one minute with a deadly accuracy, at a range of two hundred paces, and there was not an army in Christendom that could face such an assault, though as yet only the English knew the value of their astonishing weapon.

The pages had finished their cleaning and burnishing and laid out the armour in front of Sir John for his final inspection. They sighed with relief when he nodded; he was a fair and kindly master, but he was inflexible on points of cleanliness of equipment. He would never, if he could help it, go into battle with rusty armour. The pages rolled the armour in blankets as a protection against damp and dew, and Hugh went off in search of wood for the fire. He built it up and then wrapped himself in a blanket. A night in the open was no hardship to him, and he was soon asleep.

The next morning was clear and bright, with a promise of a hot day, but it was still cold when Hugh awoke, and he made up the fire again. A good day for a battle, Sir John said, warming himself by the flames. Hugh grinned. He was nervous and tense, and instinctively his head turned to the south, as it had done at regular intervals since he had woken up. But there was no sign of the French.

The camp overlooked a wide and shallow valley, with a little stream running down the centre. To the right was the small town of Crécy, and farther to the left a village called Wadicourt, so Sir John had said. The ground dropped gently to the stream, and then rose even more gradually to the skyline and the dark, green mass of the forest of Crécy, which was slightly to the right as Hugh looked across the empty valley. There was no obstacle to check the advance of the French, not even the stream, which was practically dry after the long summer.

Hugh went round the bowmen, inspecting the bows, seeing that every man had spare strings, clean helmets, and swords. The knights and men-at-arms and squires were by this time putting on their armour, a slow and methodical business. Stowed away in one of the wagons was a magnificent and very costly suit of mail and plate that Hugh had taken from the Frenchman he had shot down at Blanchetaque.

Sir John was surrounded by his pages, and Hugh sat by the fire and watched.

'The demi-jambarts, Robert,' Sir John said. The boy knelt to strap on the two plates that covered the legs. 'Too tight! That's better! Ease off the bottom strap! Good!' He stamped his feet to test the fit and ease of movement, and then another page strapped on the knee-cops; every piece had to be put on in the correct order, otherwise the next plate would not fit.

Then followed the plates over the arms, the brassart, and vambraces, and then the wide sword-belt. Twice the page adjusted the strap until Sir John was satisfied, and then he was completely armoured except for his gauntlets and bascinet, strapped and trussed in his layers of gambeson next to the skin, mail shirt, and the outer pieces of plate. It was enough to keep a man warm even on the coldest day of winter, and sufficient now to grill him on an August morning like an ox on a spit a few paces from a roaring fire, Hugh thought, sweating already in his thick brigandine.

Sir John examined his bascinet, a pig-faced one, as it was called, because of the long, pointed snout with eye-holes and breathing-holes. Strips of mail were attached to the bottom edges, falling down in folds to cover the throat and the back of the head. Hugh felt that he would be suffocated in such a helmet; his own was a much simpler affair, protecting only the top and sides of his head, and leaving the face clear, for no bowman could have drawn and loosed otherwise.

Sir James Valence and the younger knights and squires were moving about restlessly, jingling and clattering at every step, talking in bursts, and then falling silent, their heads turning every now and then towards the forest of Crécy. Hugh watched them for a moment, but he was as nervous himself, and he wandered over to the wagon park. Wat, one of the foresters who had been wounded at the ford, was sitting there, his arm in a sling as a result of a cross-bow bolt.

'Any food here, Wat?'

'Plenty of green apples, Hugh. They've given me a belly-ache. But I've two hard-boiled eggs. You can have one, Hugh.'

Hugh cracked the shell against the wheel of the wagon, and gulped down the egg hungrily. He had just finished when the trumpets sounded from the mill where the King had set up his headquarters, and Hugh ran back to the ridge. The tents were being struck, and the marshals and the commanders of the three main groups of the army were riding up and down the lines.

Sir John's company was on the extreme left wing, which was under the command of the Earl of Northampton. They were pushed slightly forward towards the slope of the valley, and all were on foot, bowmen and spearmen, knights and squires alike. Sir John and Hugh drew up the bowmen in a deep wedge, the tip well in advance so that they could loose to the front and also along the line of the heavily armoured knights. Once Sir John and Hugh were satisfied that every man knew his place, they were sent out to dig long pits about fifty paces ahead, a possible trap for horses, and others went back to bring up bundles of shafts. Each bowman had two dozen and stuck them in the ground by his place, and then refilled his quiver with another twenty or so.

The sun was overhead by this time, blazing down from a clear sky, and off came bascinets and helmets. The bowmen sat down, and all along the ridge the English army lay down and waited. Some slept, others sat in silence, and many chattered nervously. Hugh heard Sir James offer to wager one of his gold cups from Caen that the French would not come that day.

'Keep your gold plate, James,' Sir John said. 'King Philip will be here today, and all the chivalry of France behind him.'

Sir James jumped to his feet as a roar of cheering went up from the extreme right wing, and all heads turned. Riding out in front of the army was a single rider in black velvet, mounted on a white palfrey. It was King Edward. He went slowly, stopping frequently, and riding up close to the front ranks, speaking to the men, and then riding on again, leaving behind him groups of wildly cheering soldiers.

The Earl and Sir John went out to greet him as he reached the left wing. He carried no arms, Hugh noticed, only a long staff, and he smiled and nodded, and then looked long and searchingly at the bowmen and the knights as if he wished to read their thoughts and learn how much he could depend upon them that day. The brown, bearded faces, for few had shaven for days, laughed and cheered, and the King raised his hand for silence.

'I have no need to tell you to stand and fight today,' he said. 'I saw you at Caen and at the ford of Blanchetaque. King Philip will be here soon with the greatest army that he can muster behind his standard, greater than any you have yet faced.' He paused and smiled. 'All the better! The more for you bowmen to shoot down!' A chuckle went round the ranks. 'So stand and loose! Aim low for the horses! And you, gentlemen,' and he turned to the knights and squires, 'the honour of England is in your hands and swords this day. You see, all of you,' and he spread out his hands, 'this is the confidence I have in you. I shall put on no armour today. You are my armour! The army of England! St. George for England!'

Up went the spears and swords, and the bows and helmets, and as always when he was deeply moved, the King's cheeks flushed, and his dark eyes sparkled. It was, Hugh thought, the face of a great leader, an inspiring soldier, and he shouted with the rest.

They lay down again after that, and slowly the sun crawled across the sky, and over their heads; it would set behind them, Geoffrey reminded his men, and shine in the faces of the French, if they came that day. Jack spat, and grumbled that he was starving.

Nick yelped suddenly and sat up, his nose twitching. 'I can smell meat!' he said. 'Roasting meat!' He pointed towards the wagon park, and there, clear enough, was the smoke of fires rising straight up into the still air, and they could all smell that delicious scent, something they had not smelt for days. One of the squires of the company came running up to Hugh, and spoke with the respect that all of them accorded this unusual Captain of Bowmen.

'Master Fletcher,' he said, 'Sir John says that food will be brought from the wagon park. All men may fall out to collect their ration. If the trumpet sounds, they must fall in again at their places.'

Hugh jumped to his feet. 'Jack, Geoffrey! See that each man puts down his bow to mark his place. Then fall them out.'

The meat was nearly cold when it reached them, and it was tough and full of gristle. But it was roast meat, as Nick had said, and they chewed and swallowed like men who were starving, which was not far from the truth. After that they strolled about, and the tension that had been building up during the day began to disappear. Jack was arguing heatedly with another old bowman about the best type of feather for a cloth-yard shaft, and Nick was chattering excitedly. Geoffrey stretched himself out, and smiled at them placidly, and said nothing. Hugh envied him his composure. This waiting was wearing, he thought, and he could not relax.

But still the French did not come, and the army settled down once more to wait as patiently as it could. Bowmen fiddled with strings and shafts, polished helmets that were already highly burnished, or else they wandered about restlessly.

'Siddown, boy!' Jack growled at Nick. 'You keep popping up and down like a perishing rabbit! The French will come soon enough! They know where to find us.'

Nick sat down and grinned. At that moment Giles Allerton came up, holding a flagon of wine.

'There you are, Jack,' he said, and smiled his wolfish grin. 'This won't be the first time I've shared a flagon with you before a fight.' He passed it over, and sat down beside Hugh. 'You'll have to loose fast and true today, Master Hugh.'

Jack wiped his lips and spat with great satisfaction. 'There'll be so many of 'em that not even the perishing bowmen of the King's Company can miss the perishers,' he said.

'The sun will be down in a few hours,' Hugh said. 'Will they attack us if they do come today, Giles?'

'They'll attack,' Giles said. 'They'll come for us like hounds off the leash!'

When he had gone Hugh looked out thoughtfully across the wide valley. Like hounds, he thought, remembering those that Sir Henry Mortimer had loosed at them in the gorge. He had a swift vision of hundreds of baying dogs leaping at him, and he frowned. That quiet, empty valley shimmering in the heat haze, and the dark mass of the forest beyond, no longer seemed so peaceful. Suddenly it had assumed an air of menace, of brooding expectancy, waiting to disgorge sixty thousand Frenchmen, impatient to sweep down upon the tiny English force, shouting, hacking, and slashing, until they had ground them all into the blood-soaked turf. Hugh shook his head. His imagination was too vivid, and that way led to fear and panic. He put his head back and tried to sleep.

An hour later the priests who were with the army came out in front and chanted Vespers. Every man stood and bowed his head and crossed himself, and then again they sat and waited, and the sun moved farther behind them, and on the horizon some black clouds appeared.

A trumpet sounded from the mill. It was a shrill and startling blare of sound after so long a silence, and it brought everyone to their feet. A deep hum, like that of thousands of bees, went over the ridge, then shouts, and many arms pointing across the valley. Dust was drifting over the trees of the forest, and Hugh saw a quick flash of light, then another, and then a whole succession of them, swift, twinkling silvery gleams, the evening sun flashing on burnished steel and mail.

'The French!' a voice roared from behind Hugh. 'The French! Sound the trumpets! Fall in! Fall in! The French!'

14

THE BATTLE OF CRÉCY

Once the English had rushed back to take up their places in the line, the insistent trumpet-calls, the shouted orders, and the excited clamour of many voices died away, and there was almost complete silence along the whole length of the ridge, a grim, dour silence of high resolve and determination. They might well be hounds over there, as Giles had described them, a huge pack hunting down the quarry that had spoiled their lands, but the small English army was, nevertheless, a formidable and disciplined force.

It was, perhaps, like some dangerous beast of the forest, a beast gorged with plunder, who had already brushed aside with ripping fangs and claws the first clumsy and feeble attempts to drag it down. But the whole pack had sighted it now, and was baying for blood. The beast was cornered at last, and had turned sullenly to fight. There would be no mercy given by either side, when the pack leapt forward for the kill, and the quarry struck back with its sharp and far-reaching claws.

The long-bowmen, some seven thousand of them, shook themselves into a loose formation, each man making sure that he had sufficient room to draw his great bow. The slope on which they stood was a priceless advantage, as the King and his commanders had foreseen. Every bowman, even those in the second and third ranks, could loose over the heads of those in front. Seven thousand bows could fire as one.

Jack nudged Hugh and pointed to the black clouds that had reached the town of Crécy, and were moving towards the valley and the ridge.

'Ware rain!' the captains shouted. 'Cover your bows and strings! Ware rain!'

Off came the strings, to be stuffed into pouches or under helmets. Those who possessed leather cases such as Jack had made one for Hugh, wrapped their bows in those. As Hugh did that, he smiled and stroked the dark, smooth wood. Was old Watkyn the Bowyer still bent over his bench, he wondered, many hundreds of miles away? He had made a fine bow, and its greatest test had come today.

The French could be seen quite clearly now, their columns streaming out from the roads that ran through the forest, spreading out in ragged lines across the open ground on the far side of the valley, as the horsemen jostled eagerly for position. Even to a beginner in warfare such as Hugh, this was no army, only an immense mob of armoured men.

But it was a stirring and a frightening sight for all that. The whole of the ground over there was soon crammed with a mass of horsemen, and there were many on foot, too, cross-bowmen, so Hugh assumed, and drawn up in a more orderly formation than the horsemen. The banners and pennons waved over a restless sea of helmets and the tossing heads of many thousands of horses. The clamour of that great host, the clatter and the jingle of armour and harness, the incessant calls of trumpets, the shouts and cheers of brave men impatient to charge their enemy, rose in an angry and menacing roar that rolled across the wide valley towards the silent and motionless army of King Edward.

Coldly and stolidly the English watched this great gathering of the chivalry of France, arrayed there against them with such pride and an exultant courage, under the banners of their feudal lords, the tall standards of Burgundy and Aquitaine, of Picardy and Vendôme, Gascony and Lorraine and Poitou, all following with a reckless fury the royal Oriflamme of France.

Hugh saw isolated horsemen trotting across the front of this seething crowd, trying to bring some order and plan into the chaos, he thought. But it was a hopeless task. As each fresh contingent emerged from the forest, and saw the English in the distance, the riders brandished their spears, and one group galloped immediately down the slope until they were halted and persuaded to fall back in line with the others.

Then six columns of men on foot began to move forward, marching steadily and in a regular formation.

'Cross-bows,' Jack muttered. 'Genoese cross-bowmen. They'll wish they'd never left Italy before we've finished with 'em!' He spat contemptuously.

Hugh watched the columns and tried to make a guess at the number. 'Quite six thousand,' he said, and Jack nodded and agreed, a far greater force of Genoese than the long-bows had ever faced before. They respected the cross-bow; it was accurate, and had a long range. But its rate of fire was slow. After

each bolt the bow had to be brought down, and the thick cord rewound with a small ratchet, and a good long-bowman could loose three shafts in that time.

A deep rumble of thunder rolled sullenly across the valley, and all heads went up. The black clouds were directly over the stream, swallowing up the sunlight, and spreading a chilly gloom over the two armies. Lightning flickered eerily against the sombre background.

'What's that?' Jack cried, and in his hoarse voice was a note of fear that Hugh had never heard there before.

The air was filled with the croakings of hundreds of birds. Great flocks of carrion-crows flapped clumsily out of the forest as if they were trying to escape in a blind panic from the threat of the approaching storm; or perhaps they had been alarmed by the march of the enormous French army through the forest. They passed slowly over the English ranks, croaking dismally, swaying and dipping in their ungainly flight, many waves of large, black birds, as sinister and ill-omened a sight as any man could have imagined just before a great battle.

Jack's brown face had gone a chalky white. He crossed himself several times, and muttered inaudible prayers. Even Geoffrey was frowning, and Nick, head back, stared upwards, his mouth wide open. Hugh shook his head, but he could not fight down a feeling of superstitious awe and foreboding.

'Well, here's my last fight,' Jack said.

'Don't be a fool, Jack!' Geoffrey said sharply. 'Haven't you seen a flock of carrion-crows before?'

'I've always hated the perishers,' Jack said. 'An old witch told me once they'd be the death of me. And there they are.'

A vicious streak of lightning flashed across the front of the bowmen. Hugh flinched and stepped back a pace. Above his head the thunder crackled and ripped, and he heard the sound of the rain sweeping across the valley. Hurriedly he fastened the thongs of his bow case, and then the storm burst upon them, hissing and pattering on the ground and the steel helmets, drenching and chilly after the heat of the sun, and blotting out the sight of the French army and the advancing cross-bowmen with a grey curtain of driving water.

The heavens exploded in a maddened and gigantic inferno of light and noise. The incessant flashes of lightning and the bellowing roar of the thunder seemed to be tearing the skies apart. The English soldiers cowered below the storm, terrified by this appalling uproar, as if they realized that nature was intent on showing them how puny the squabbles of mere humans were compared to this stupendous display of power and limitless violence.

For ten minutes or so Hugh crouched on the ground, dazed and awed, and then as suddenly as it had come, the storm drifted away. The black clouds had gone and the sun shone warmly on the green turf, the grass sparkling with raindrops, while in the distance the thunder still boomed out with a sullen fury.

'Bows out! Brace your bows! Stand and nock! Stand and nock!'

It was Sir John Carey, and Hugh jumped to his feet. The shouts of the captains of bowmen, and his own voice as he fell in with the foresters sounded shrill and thin after the deafening rumble of the thunder. He went round the deep wedge to see that every string was dry and taut, and then he returned to his place and braced his own bow, his sodden hose clammy and cold against his skin. Water was trickling down his neck beneath his brigandine and shirt, and he shivered and shook himself like a great hound.

He adjusted the leather brassart on his left forearm as a protection against the whip of the string, and pulled on a thin leather mitten on the fingers of his right hand. Normally he never wore one, for his skin was hard and calloused after years of pulling a bowstring. But he knew that today he would probably loose more shafts in a few hours than he had ever done in so short a time. He checked to see that all had two dozen shafts ready in the ground, that their quivers were filled, and that the bundles of spare shafts were placed where they could be fetched without any delay.

'Here they come,' Geoffrey said quietly. Even now, at this

supreme moment, he was calm and stolid, and Hugh envied him. He was an immense and formidable figure in his helmet and brigandine, holding a bow longer than any in the whole company. Hugh looked at him and smiled, and then he turned to face the rest of the bowmen. As he saw the brown faces, burnt almost black by the sun, unshaven, the firm mouths, and the steady eyes watchful and fixed on the advancing Genoese as they marched briskly up the slope, he knew that he could stand his ground and loose all day before these men would turn and run. The French, if they overran the ridge, would spare the knights and the squires for the sake of their ransoms. But the bowmen would be cut down mercilessly. They all knew that, and they waited with a grim and stolid determination, masters of their deadly weapons. They knew, too, what the French and Genoese had yet to learn, that they could massacre every man advancing up that slope.

The Genoese halted by the stream, and deployed from their long columns into line across the full width of the English position. Their captains shouted, and they marched forward again, across the stream, shook themselves with a practised precision into regular lines, and came on up the easy slope. They were within range of the long-bows, and had been for some time, but up above them the experienced captains of bowmen and the commanders of the English wings waited grimly.

The Genoese halted. They waved their stumpy weapons in the air, and shouted:

'St. Denis! Ho! St. Denis! Ho!'

Twice they repeated this cheer, a deep roar of defiance from six thousand men, and from far behind them the French trumpets screamed, and all the impatient horsemen shook their lances and yelled their encouragement. But the long-bowmen stood motionless; each great bow pointed to the ground, and on each string rested a slim shaft with its smooth, tapering tip of hardened steel. Every face had set hard, and they watched the cross-bowmen in a cold and forbidding silence. A single trumpet sounded from the centre of the line, and a disciplined rustle passed along the wedges as each man slid forward his left foot. Fingers tightened on the strings, and the bowmen of England were ready.

Up in the mill behind them King Edward leant forward, his long, white hands gripping the wooden rail. The decisive moment had come for him, perhaps the most momentous of his long life. Within a few minutes the fate of his army would be settled, the future of his kingdom, and his place in history. Only the tightening of his fingers on the rough wood showed his feelings. Had he made a disastrous mistake, an irretrievable miscalculation when he decided to stand and fight against enormous odds? Or was he right, he and his most experienced commanders down there under the standards of the English chivalry, when they believed that the massed fire from thousands of bowmen would revolutionize the art of warfare, and mow down the traditional winners of all battles, the charge of the heavily armoured knights on horseback?

The Genoese halted for the last time. Hugh heard the shrill, staccato orders in a language he did not understand. Up came the cross-bows. A horde of short, thick bolts hummed up into the air. Hugh braced himself for the searing shock of the impact, and closed his eyes for a second. Crossing the ford at Blanchetaque was a child's game compared to this onslaught. His hand closed convulsively on the grip of his bow, and he looked up, his whole body ready to flinch as the bolts came down. To his intense surprise they were all falling short, and well short, too, plunging harmlessly into the sodden ground. Like all the other bowmen he realized immediately what had happened; that lashing rainstorm had soaked the cords of the cross-bows. Too late the Genoese realized their mistake; and they all bent down, feet on the bow, rewinding the cords like madmen. Perhaps they knew how fatal and suicidal that mistake had been.

Not one trumpet from the French side this time, but many sounded from the English lines, shrilly, urgently, and triumphantly. The long bows came up all along the ridge, and the strings whipped forward with a resonant hum. Seven thousand shafts whistled down the slope; to many who watched from the lines of the knights and men-at-arms it seemed as if a sudden blizzard of snow was driving across the valley, so thick was the stream of shafts with their grey and white feathers.

But the bowmen had not paused to watch the flight. Like

Hugh, the moment the shaft had left the string, they had brought down the bow and snatched up the next shaft. This was no time for careful target practice, with a leisurely inspection of the aim and range; this was a frantic matter of life or death: kill and massacre the Genoese, or be impaled on those thick, hard-driven bolts. They had drawn and loosed again before that first wave had reached their marks, and they could not possibly miss at that short range. For a third time they nocked and drew, and another hissing storm of feathered shafts swept over the green slopes. The trumpets blew, and the great bows came down, and the hard-breathing bowmen looked anxiously to their front.

In that frantic minute nearly twenty thousand shafts had been hurled at the wretched Genoese, at a range of no more than a hundred and fifty paces, each steel point driven with a fearful velocity ripping through leather coats and mail shirts, a ceaseless hail of death. The cross-bowmen had gone; they lay in orderly lines on the ground from one end of the ridge to the other, twisted, untidy bundles, most quite still, many still writhing in agony. The survivors had turned and were racing down the hill, throwing away their useless weapons, heads down and shoulders hunched, dreading the sound of the whistling shafts that might pursue them. But none did. The English commanders had no wish to waste valuable ammunition. Not all the gold that King Philip could offer would have persuaded those cross-bowmen to march again against those frightful long-bows.

From the main body of the French army there went up a howl of rage that could be heard quite clearly by the English. The French chivalry had waited reluctantly for the Genoese to make the first attack, for they could not see the necessity for any delay before they themselves charged and rode over this handful of men on foot. Waves of horsemen galloped forward without waiting for any orders. Hugh saw them hack down with swords and maces at the running Genoese, and the charge, disorderly enough at the start, became a ragged wave of reckless men.

They flooded across the stream, thousands of them, the drum of hooves as loud, it seemed to the waiting English, as the

thunder of the storm, and the sheer sight of that tremendous mass of men as they spurred up the slope was more frightening and awe-inspiring than anything that Hugh or most of those on the ridge had ever seen.

Hugh's stomach turned; his throat was dry, and he could feel his knees quivering. Standing, as he did, at the front of the wedge of bowmen, he had no protection, no thick ditch or a castle wall behind which he could cower. He was on foot, exposed and in the open, and with only a bow to ward off the French. As he watched the thousands of horses canter up the slope, without a single break in the long lines, and with a dense, swarming mass in the rear, he felt it was impossible to check, even for a moment, that tremendous weight of horses and heavily armoured men, in bascinet and mail and plate, holding long lances, swords, and maces. The bravest of men, he thought, would have stared in horror, and at that moment he was a very frightened young man.

'Aim low!' Jack muttered. 'For the horses!'

Hugh nodded, and swallowed hard before he turned and shouted his orders.

'Aim for the horses! Aim low!'

The cry was taken up by the knights who stood waiting on either side of the wedges.

'Stand fast! Aim for the horses! Stand fast!'

Some of the French knights had drawn clear of the rest, and were forcing their horses to a gallop up the slope. They had settled down in their saddles for the last dash, lances firm, only the tops of their helmets showing above the shield. The Earl of Northampton and Sir John Carey were standing just behind the men-at-arms, bascinets open, watching intently. They were veterans, but they had never faced such a charge as this. The Earl's eyes turned to Sir John, who nodded.

'Sound!' the Earl said sharply.

His trumpeter drew a deep breath; his cheeks bulged and his face went crimson with his efforts. If it had been his choice he would have blown long ago, and his frantic urgency and alarm went into that call as he blew as he had never blown before.

'Draw!' Hugh bellowed. 'Draw and loose!'

The leading horsemen were no more than a hundred paces distant now, and were picking up speed as the tired horses were spurred on mercilessly for the last charge. The thunder of the hooves deepened, and above it Hugh could hear the jangle of mail and harness, and the shrill yells of the French knights:

'St. Denis! St. Denis!'

Hugh drew and loosed. His shaft shot away and was lost immediately in the hundreds that surrounded it, swooping over the slope, the flight almost flat. He nocked and drew again, and then for a third time, before the Earl's trumpeter sounded the cease fire.

Hugh let out his breath in a long sigh, and lowered his bow. The chivalry of France, so confident and brave, in all the glory of their pennons and painted shields, with the proud arms of their families on their jupons and surcoats, mounted on magnificent chargers, had become a shambles. A wall of kicking, rearing horses had sprung in front of the bowmen; helpless riders were pinned beneath, suffocated in their bascinets, or with broken limbs. Many horses had turned violently, their chests and flanks tortured by the thin shafts that had been driven deep into them, and had collided in their frenzy with those pressing on from the rear; more had fallen into the pits, and those following had piled up on top in a hideous heap of neighing horses and shrieking men.

But some had escaped, and were still riding hard for the steady lines of English knights, swerving away from the wedges of the bowmen. One man was heading straight for the foresters.

'Jack! Geoffrey! Loose with me!'

Hugh drew almost leisurely. That first terrible feeling of tension and fear had gone. He brought up his left hand, the knuckles level with the chest of the horse, the great bow at full stretch, and loosed. On each side of him the bows twanged, and three shafts whirred away, converging on the galloping horse, no more than fifty paces away now. The animal reared up and fell on its side, and its rider went with it, the bascinet hitting the ground with a metallic clash, and there he lay, his leg pinned under the dead horse, stunned, Hugh thought, by his fall.

'He! He!' the foresters shouted, and Jack spat with much satisfaction.

Sir John walked forward, and looked along the front ranks. But everywhere the scene was the same, the heaps of horses and riders, all along the ridge from one end to the other. Those Frenchmen who had been at the rear of that first charge, had escaped the worst of the arrow storm, and they were riding back across the stream.

'Fetch your shafts!' Sir John yelled. 'Fall in when the trumpet sounds.'

The bowmen rushed out, and with them went the knights and squires. Shafts were precious, but there were prisoners out there, and one ransom would keep a bowman in comfort and security for the rest of his life, and pay all the debts of some needy squire, or perhaps even buy a small manor.

'Ours!' Jack growled, bending over the horse they had just shot down. 'Keep off, curse you!' He had his dagger out, and a young squire, who had run out with them recoiled hastily. Where a fat ransom was at stake, men would knife each other without any hesitation. Geoffrey and Hugh heaved at the dead horse, and Jack pulled the Frenchman clear. He was unwounded, and was fumbling with the front of his bascinet. It was a young face that emerged, flushed and anxious as he looked up at the three brown, bearded faces above him.

'I am Raoul de Goncourt, messieurs,' he said, and Hugh and

Geoffrey understood the French, for it was spoken commonly enough by the noblemen of England. 'I will gladly pay you a fair ransom for my life.'

'You will!' Jack said. 'Up! Walk!'

'Take him back to the wagon park,' Hugh said. 'Wat will keep guard. We'll pick up shafts.'

They ran forward to the line of dead and wounded horses. Hundreds of English soldiers, bowmen and knights, were bending over Frenchmen, ripping open bascinets, cursing furiously when they found the man was dead, or shouting with delight at a wounded man, and snarling like dogs at anyone they thought might steal their prisoner. Hugh and Geoffrey pulled up two armfuls of shafts in the turf, and then the trumpets blew, and they all turned and scampered back to their posts.

The French were attacking again, the same untidy lines, many deep, flooding slowly across the stream and cantering up the slope, with the same dash and reckless confidence as those who had made the first charge. But the ground was littered now with the ruins of that attack, and the canter became a trot as the French tried to jostle for position at the gaps.

'Hold!' Hugh shouted. 'Wait until they bunch at the gaps!'

He saw Sir John, who was standing close by the bowmen. He had heard Hugh's order, and he nodded.

'Loose when you wish,' he said.

There was one gap immediately in front of the foresters, and Hugh ran forward, and pointed with his bow. The helmeted heads of the foresters nodded briefly.

'Draw!' The French were pouring through the gap, and the leading riders were deploying to right and left.

'Loose!'

A torrent of shafts converged on that narrow target, not only from Sir John's company, but from the wedge just to their right. Hugh loosed twice, glancing briefly at the mass of horses; he heard the distinctive clang of the shafts crashing into mail and plate, the whinny of frightened and wounded horses, and the yells of the French knights. There was not a moment when the air was not filled with the whistle of those shafts until the Earl gestured to his trumpeter. There was no longer a gap, only a heap of men and horses.

Hugh wiped his face. He was streaming with perspiration, and all his body seemed on fire with the heat. His hose, drenched by the storm, had dried under the hot sun, and he pulled off his helmet and wiped away the sweat that trickled down into his eyes.

Again the English broke their ranks and rushed forward in search of shafts and prisoners. Hugh tore open a fat saddle-bag on a dead horse. There was bread and meat there, and a purse filled with gold coins. Nick waved a flagon of wine, and Hugh gulped it down thirstily, and then tore at the meat with his strong teeth. Never had food and drink tasted so delicious, he thought, and he grinned at Nick.

The French charged again, and for the next hour perhaps, for Hugh lost all sense of time, the pattern of the battle was the same. He drew and loosed; the horses fell or swerved away, and were hit by fresh shafts; the riders fell, and the English surged forward, dragging back their prisoners, and reforming their steady lines once more as another French charge came up the slope. As for the knights, they had done no fighting yet. The French had never reached them.

But one charge broke through against the centre of the army. Hugh, at the front of the wedge, could see the two lines close, the French hacking down at the English knights who stabbed and thrust with lance and sword. He heard the deep shouts of men fighting desperately, and the clatter and screech of steel on steel, as if a hundred blacksmiths were at work. Then the line was clear, and a storm of shafts fell on the French as they retreated, and the centre was in line, the English waving their swords in triumph.

The sun was sinking fast, throwing long shadows over the ground. But the battle had barely begun, Sir John said to Hugh.

The other side of the valley was still crowded with French knights, and more columns were emerging from the forest, all eager to rush into the fight. The evening sun still glittered on the helmets and the armour, and each fresh arrival shouted and rode down the slope towards the ridge. They could not believe that a mere handful of footmen could stand against the chivalry of France; they were brave men, and so long as there was light to see they would charge.

'Ware right! To the right!'

French horsemen had trotted through a narrow gap, and rode for the men-at-arms facing them. The nearest wedge of bowmen were loosing to their right, and the French came on unchecked. They charged home against the line of the knights and squires, and the English reeled back in a flurry of breaking lances, and wildly swinging swords. Hugh held up his hand. It was almost impossible to shoot for fear of hitting their own men, and they watched helplessly, as the two groups were completely entangled in a confused and shifting mass. But the English held. Their bellows of 'St. George!' were answered by the yells of 'St. Denis! Montjoie!' and the French began to deploy along their front.

'Pick your men!' Hugh yelled. 'Loose when you can!'

The French carried their shields on their left, and their right sides were unprotected against the arrows that flickered past the English. The hard-driven shafts thudded into the horses, clinked and cracked up against the mail of the riders, and the English surged forward again to straighten their ranks.

One Frenchman, almost completely encased in plate armour, his bascinet crowned with a tall plume, his surcoat and shield bright with blue and gold designs, had bent low in his saddle. He pulled his horse round to face the arrows, and spurred for them. His lance had snapped, and he was holding a mace, a long, thick shaft ending in a solid ball of steel with projecting points, a fearful weapon, for where a sword might do no more than dent a piece of plate or the top of a helmet, this would by its sheer weight smash and crush the bones beneath the strongest armour.

One English knight ran out and hacked at him with his sword. The Frenchman hardly checked his pace. He leant over and swung down his ponderous mace with an easy and murderous skill. It landed full on the knight's bascinet with a dull clang, and he went down in a heap and without a sound, his helmet split from front to back, the visor torn loose by that dreadful blow.

Hugh had drawn. At barely thirty paces he loosed straight

for the horse. Up went its head as the shaft tore into its chest, but its rider held him on its course with a grim persistence. Hugh grunted and snatched up another shaft. But he knew there was no time. His fingers fumbled on the string as he stared in a sickening horror at that steel-clad monster rushing at him, the long mace swinging up slowly, and the arm going back to its full length for a blow that would shatter his thin helmet and every bone in his skull.

From his side came a hoarse yell. Jack jumped forward, the string back to his ear. The shaft hit the Frenchman's bascinet slightly to one side as he ducked his head. The steel point slithered over the hardened and curved surface with a screech, and down came the mace, a blur of merciless death. It landed full on Jack's helmet with the sullen clang of a sledge-hammer pounding a solid bar of iron.

Jack's knees bent, and he dropped slowly. Another shaft drove into the horse, and it reared up, kicking out frantically with its forefeet. One caught Hugh and sent him sprawling back on the ground, and then the horse collapsed on its side. The knight threw himself clear, but he had dropped his mace. He came to one knee, his right hand groping for his weapon, half blinded by the thin eye-slits of his bascinet.

Geoffrey was standing over Jack. He kicked aside the gaunt-leted hand that was within an inch of the mace, snatched it up with both hands, and swung it down from his great height with a bellow of fury. The hinged front of the Frenchman's helmet was crumpled and smashed, and Geoffrey roared again, and brought down the mace for the second time.

Hugh turned Jack over gently. One glance was enough, and he groaned. One part of his life had ended with Jack; he had grown up in the forest, and in a sense old Jack had been a father to him.

'It was my fault, Geoffrey,' he said. 'I was too slow.'

'It was nobody's fault. Pick up your bow, Hugh. We've not finished yet.'

Hugh went back to his place. The French had been pushed back by the men-at-arms, and the left wing was clear. Two Frenchmen on foot were walking away, one limping badly, and the other holding him up.

'Those two,' Hugh muttered. 'Take the one limping, Geoffrey.'

They nocked slowly, and came up to the aim carefully and deliberately. There was no need for haste, and they might have been at the butts in the forest. Hugh brought the knuckles of his hand level with the helmet of his man, and held his breath as Jack had taught him years ago. He did not hear Geoffrey loose, so intent was he on a perfect shot. But he saw the two shafts, almost side by side, and he heard the crack as they hit the backs of the two men. Coldly and without pity he watched them stagger under the impact, arms up, sprawling forward on their faces, with the feathers of the shafts sticking up triumphantly in the centre of each back.

There was a pause after that in the attacks against the left wing. When the French did advance, their main effort was on the right of the English, where the Prince of Wales was commanding. This was a determined charge, not one wave of riders, but a dense mass, sixty or seventy deep, and though the first ranks went down, the others pressed on through the incessant fire of the bows, and came to grips with the men-at-arms. For half an hour the rest of the army watched and listened anxiously to that fierce struggle. But gradually the longbows picked off the horses and the riders, and the men-at-arms stood fast, though they had been pushed back from the crest of the ridge. At last Hugh saw the French break and turn away, while a torrent of arrows caught them as they trotted down the slope. The right wing reformed, and the English trumpets sounded defiantly as the standard of the Prince was carried forward once more.

Hugh drank some wine that he had taken from a French saddle-bag, and all the foresters had done the same, so there was no lack of food for them. Hugh's legs were aching, and the muscles of his arms and back were tiring from the continual strain of drawing his great bow. But there was little chance of a rest, for the French attacks were persistent.

The bottom of the valley was in deep shadow, and a mist was drifting over the line of the stream. But above they could still see the French, and there seemed to be as many horsemen as there had been when the battle began. Wearily Hugh ordered fresh bundles of shafts to be brought up and pointed to the extreme left where a large body of French was coming up the hill.

As they reached the top of the slope and emerged from the darkness of the valley into the last of the evening sunlight, their armour suddenly flashed and glittered like silver; their armorial bearings on shield and jupon changed magically from dull patterns to gaily painted and embroidered pictures and designs, strangely beautiful, Hugh thought, as the trumpets screamed and the familiar drum of hooves rolled over the hard ground.

But there was no sense of beauty as they came closer. These

men seemed hardly human with their blank faces of smooth steel, even more cold and sinister in the half-light. Hugh braced himself as he nocked a shaft. He forgot the ache in his legs and arms, and the tiredness of his fingers, strained as they had never been before by the intense pull of the string and the strong limbs of his bow.

'Draw and loose!' he shouted. There was no need for trumpet-calls now to control the fire of the bowmen. They knew exactly what they had to do, and how best to drive off each attack. Hugh drew and aimed mechanically, without picking any special target. At that range, and with the French riding so close together, neither he nor any of the others could miss hitting something, horse or man.

The first wave was smashed, and the rest split up into small groups, picking their way past the dead horses, and advancing wherever there was a gap. Fifty or sixty reached the spearmen. One horse fell, and knocked over a file of men, and the riders behind crashed through the opening. The whole of the left wing recoiled, and the bowmen were helpless.

'Right!' Geoffrey bellowed. 'To the right!'

Hugh turned. He had been watching Sir John Carey fling himself into the gap, sword raised, bending down behind his shield. Another scattered charge was coming from the right, and the light was so bad now that it was difficult to pick a target. A maddened and riderless horse rode into Geoffrey, and sent him flying. Hugh jumped aside just in time, and then a horse loomed above him, and a tall, dark figure in the saddle, arm upraised.

A tremendous blow came down on the top of his helmet. He was conscious of the screech of the sword, and a scarlet flame seemed to flash across his eyes. He shook his head, his strong legs keeping him upright. He saw the blur of a white surcoat above him, and jumped forward, arms out, for he had dropped his bow and there was no time to draw a sword. He gripped the top of the man's shield, and tugged backwards with all his weight. The Frenchman yelled, and tried to hack at Hugh's head, but already he was being dragged from his saddle, and down he came with a clatter of mail. Two bowmen leapt astride of him, swords raised. But Hugh shouted at them.

'Prisoner!' he yelled. 'Ransom, you fools!'

Nick tugged at the front of the curved bascinet, and a white face peered up at them.

'He's alive,' Nick said. 'Your prisoner, Hugh.'

'That makes two for you,' Geoffrey said. 'Head hurt?'

Hugh took off his helmet. His head was still ringing, and there was a long dent in the helmet, but no bones were broken. The attack had been beaten back by the spearmen and the knights led by Sir John, who had filled the gap. It was quite dark now, Hugh realized. The sun had gone down, and the moon was just appearing over the forest.

Sir John clanked up to them, with Sir James by his side. Both carried signs of that last fight, ripped jupons, a dent in Sir John's bascinet, and a long, jagged scar across the front of his shield.

'How is it with the bowmen, Hugh?' Sir John asked.

'Jack's dead, my lord.'

'Jack Cherryman! How did that happen?' He nodded sadly as Hugh told him the story. 'Well, it was how he would have chosen,' he said.

One of his squires had just appeared, and was touching Sir John's arm.

'My lord, my lord! Sir Henry Mortimer! He would have word with you.'

'Well, I would not,' Sir John said curtly.

'He is dying, my lord.'

Sir John hesitated. 'I cannot refuse that,' he said. 'You come, too, Hugh. The French will not attack again for a time.'

'But won't they retreat now that the sun's down?' Hugh asked as they made their way to the rear.

'I doubt it. We shall have a few more hours of it.'

Sir Henry was lying on the ground by one of the wagons, and two of his squires were standing close by, one holding a torch. They had stripped off some of his armour, and across his chest was a long tear in the mail. His face, always white Hugh remembered, was almost bloodless now, thin and haggard in the flickering glare of the torch. His eyes were open, and they moved up slowly to look at Sir John.

'When you return to Grosmont, Sir John,' he muttered, 'I pray you to visit my wife.'

'What do you wish me to say, Henry?'

Sir Henry's thin lips moved faintly in a smile, and Hugh knew why. Sir John had told him that they had once been squires together, and for a time were close friends.

'Pray her to forgive me, John,' he said.

'I will gladly do that. Is there anything else I can do for you now, Henry?'

'Nothing. I am bleeding to death.'

Sir John nodded, stood there for a moment, and then moved slowly away.

'He was an evil man,' he said to Hugh. 'And yet, I suppose, there must be some good in every man.' He sighed. 'There will be much for the Lady Mortimer to forgive. Still, it may give her some comfort. She is related to me, Hugh.'

The mist was creeping up from the valley, and the pauses between the French charges were longer. But still they came, the cold light of the moon glinting on their armour, while the weary bowmen drew and loosed into the night at the dark shapes as they swept over the ridge. Hugh drew with the rest, exhausted now, and it was an effort to pull back the string, and his fingers were trembling as he nocked a fresh shaft, and braced himself for the tug of the bow.

Then for a long time there was no charge at all, and the English knew that they had won the battle, and that the French would not attack them again that night.

Sentries were posted well in front of the ridge, and the knights and the bowmen lay down where they had stood all day, too tired to speak, and only asking for a chance to rest and sleep.

Hugh stretched himself out beside Geoffrey. The grass was damp with dew, and he shivered, for it was cold now after the heat of the day. He put his head on his quiver and closed his eyes.

15
THE GOLDEN SPURS

Hugh awoke with a start. He sat up and stared about him, wondering for a moment where he was. A white mist hung over him, and he saw figures moving, and heard the hum of voices, and an occasional trumpet-call. He stood up and stretched himself painfully. His head was aching, and his whole body was stiff and cold. He was extremely hungry, too, and he searched in his pack for some food, hoping that he had left a little there. He found a small piece of meat and dry bread, and a few mouthfuls of wine.

Geoffrey was still lying down, examining his right leg where the hose was torn and blood-stained. He shook his head when Hugh offered to tie up the wound, grunting moodily that it was no more than a scratch. His face was drawn and tired, with deep lines running from his nose to the corners of his mouth. However, it was not exhaustion, Hugh guessed, but sorrow, for Geoffrey had been devoted to Jack.

The mist covered the ridge and the valley, and it was impossible to see for much more than twenty paces. Dead horses and sprawling figures of men lay scattered over the wet grass in front of the English position, and bowmen and spearmen were wandering about in search of loot and food.

'Ah, there you are, Hugh.' It was Sir John, his jupon torn and his armour streaked with rust. Sir James was with him, stamping his feet, and cursing the mist and the chill of the morning.

'Fall in the bowmen, Hugh, and bring up the horses.'

'Are we moving so soon, my lord?'

'Not yet. The King has ordered the Earl to take forward a detachment of mounted bowmen and a company of knights to see what has become of the French. You will be in command of all the bowmen, including the Earl's men. Report to me when you are ready to move off.'

The business of collecting the horses, checking the supply of shafts, inspecting bows and strings, kept Hugh occupied for over half an hour, and he forgot his stiffness and cold. The mist was lifting slowly, and when they rode down into the valley, he could see two other companies riding away to the far right of the line. There were three parties altogether, Sir John explained, one from each section of the army.

As they rode down the hill, they passed the dreadful litter of a great battle. The ground was covered with the debris of a defeated army, discarded swords and shields, lances, helmets, pieces of armour, and torn, mud-stained banners and pennons. Everywhere there were horses, many still moving painfully, and that to Hugh, who loved horses, was the worst sight of all.

There were dead men, too, in every conceivable posture, stiff and ungainly, and a hundred paces away the long regular lines of the Genoese cross-bowmen, mown down as they tried to rewind their weapons, by those first murderous volleys of the long-bows.

Over all this ghastly scene were the long, feathered shafts, in horses and men, standing up on every yard of ground, like some unnatural and loathsome weed that had sprung up during the night. Men were moving about through the shambles, stripping the valuable armour from the bodies, searching saddle-bags for money and loot. But there were others more merciful, the monks who were with the army, helping the wounded, and the clerks from the King's household, counting the dead, noting the bearings on shield and jupon, and making long lists on sheets of parchment.

There was little need to count, Hugh thought. Anyone could see for himself that King Edward had shattered the French army, and had won a victory so decisive that the news of it would resound throughout Christendom, and with it the name of the long-bow that had massacred the greatest army that France had ever put into the field.

The Earl led his column across the stream, and up the slope towards the forest of Crécy. Up there the ground was clear of the dead, though there were horses in plenty, and a considerable quantity of equipment, thrown away or lost during the night, sufficient evidence of the hurried retreat of the French.

Hugh rode at the head of the bowmen, and looked about warily as they took a narrow road through the trees. He disliked this march through such a confined space where the bowmen could not make full use of their weapons, and especially when they were on horseback.

'What is it, Hugh?' Sir John asked. 'You should be at home in a forest.'

'I am, sir. But we need room to use our bows. And the bowmen should be on foot. Let me lead with the foresters. We know what to look for.'

'That makes good sense.' Sir John cantered up to the head of the column, and the Earl nodded and raised his hand for the knights to halt.

Hugh had followed, and caught at the trumpeter's arm. 'No trumpet-calls, my lord,' he said. 'The French will hear us, if they are near.'

The Earl smiled. 'You have a head on your shoulders, Master Fletcher. Have it your own way then.' He turned to one of his squires. 'Richard, ride back and bid the bowmen dismount. Leave twenty of them with the horses. Master Fletcher, take the lead when you are ready, and we will follow fifty paces or more behind you.'

Hugh hesitated, and Sir John bent down from his saddle. 'What else, Hugh?' he asked.

'I would have some more bowmen in the rear, my lord. It is easy to lay an ambush in the forest.'

The Earl looked at Sir John, his dark brows rising in inquiry, but he was smiling.

'He is teaching us our business, John. But he is right. You have laid an ambush of your own in a forest, I remember.'

Hugh grinned. 'Yes, my lord.'

He sent back the horses, and fell in the foresters three deep, with sufficient space between the files for them to draw and loose without any delay. The road was straight and level, and the trees came to within fifteen paces of the verge. There were many traces of the French retreat, the thousands of hoof marks on the turf each side of the road, and at regular intervals more dead horses, and the black ashes of camp fires.

They marched steadily for about a mile before Hugh held up his hand and pointed. The Earl and Sir John rode up to join him. To the left was a grass-covered ride leading into the depths of the forest, and marked by the telltale hoof marks. Hugh bent down over the horse droppings; they were fresh and warm.

'Well, John?' the Earl said.

'Push on carefully,' Sir John said. 'We shall hear them soon enough if they are near the road. They can't charge through these trees.'

'Cross-bows?' the Earl asked.

Sir John laughed. 'Those Genoese won't face our long-bows again, William.'

They moved off again, all eyes on the trees to the left, but they had not covered more than a quarter of a mile before the ground suddenly opened out into a wide clearing dotted with bushes, and rising gradually to higher ground about five-hundred paces distant. Hugh halted, and cocked his head, listening intently. He was accustomed to the normal sounds of a forest, the breeze rustling in the upper branches of the trees as it was that morning, and the calls of the birds, but he was waiting for the unusual, and he heard it, though very faintly, a distant jingle and a subdued clatter.

'Horsemen, my lord,' he said to the Earl.

'They're behind that high ground,' Sir John said. 'Look!'

A single figure on horseback appeared against the skyline, and his armour twinkled briefly in the sun before he vanished again. Almost immediately they heard the shrill notes of a trumpet.

'John!' the Earl said. 'Form up the knights and men-at-arms in four lines. The bowmen in the centre. No man is to charge unless my trumpeter sounds. Let the bowmen do their work first, and then we will show these French knights that we can fight on horseback as well as on foot!'

Hugh ran down the line, and drew up the bowmen in three lines. They were all veterans by now, and fell in quickly. Without any need for further orders they pulled out their shafts, stuck them ready into the ground, and shook themselves out into a loose formation.

Sir John reined in beside Hugh, who had stationed himself on the extreme right of the bowmen. He smiled at Hugh, and then pulled down the front of his bascinet with a clang, and shook his lance in the air, feeling the balance. Hugh grinned. He was feeling tense, but with none of that sensation of near panic he had experienced when the French had attacked the previous day. He glanced at the bowmen, but there was no need there for him to worry. They knew, too, that they had the measure of any French charge.

The men-at-arms were drawn up by this time in long, shifting lines, the banners of the Earl and the bannerets fluttering in the breeze. Every face was hidden behind steel; the surcoats and jupons were stained and torn, the armour streaked with rust. As for the bowmen, they had not shaved or changed their clothes for days. They were a ragged collection of men, their helmets rusty, their hose filthy. But all down the line, the swords were clean, the bows well waxed and the strings supple.

Hugh nocked a shaft, and pushed out his left leg. Suddenly he realized that Jack was no longer by his side, spitting loudly, and making rude comments in his hoarse voice; nor was Geoffrey there, for his leg wound had kept him with the wagons. But Nick was chattering busily, and grinned happily at Hugh.

A buzz of excited shouts went along the English line as trumpets sounded in the distance. The skyline was suddenly broken up as if by magic as a line of horsemen trotted into view, and swept towards the road. They came at an easy canter at first, covering the full width of the clearing, and twenty or thirty deep. The trumpets called again, and the canter became a gallop, with the familiar drum of hooves, the jingle and clatter of armour, and the long lances came down for the charge.

Two riders had broken clear of the rest, galloping ahead at a furious pace. Several bows came up, and Hugh shouted. He wanted no wasted or hasty fire.

'Nick, you loose at the one on the left with me! Walter, Roger, take the man on the right. Draw!'

Hugh came up slowly to the aim, and as the horse reached a bush he had marked, he loosed, and Nick followed suit. As the shaft left the string, he snatched up another, but there was no need. The horse, a big bay, was swerving away, its rider fighting to control it, and the right-hand rider had already been thrown by his wounded horse.

The main charge opened out slightly to avoid the two horses, and came on at a gallop. Hugh waited calmly. When they reach that line of gorse-bushes, he was muttering to himself. His arm raised, he ran forward a few paces so that all the bowmen could see him. As he started to bring his arm down, so all the bows came up. The French did not falter as they saw that menacing sight, but their courage did not help them. There was the same familiar sight to which the bowmen were accustomed by now. Their first volley halted the charge stone-dead, with wounded and frightened horses, and the second wave of shafts increased the chaos.

The Earl nodded to his trumpeter. But the English knights were already on the move. They had fought on foot all day at Crécy, and now was their chance to ride into battle as they had been taught. They surged forward with a deep roar of 'St. George!' and smashed into the stationary ranks of the French with an irresistible force and fury that swept away the remnants of the French knights in a headlong flight.

The bowmen stood and watched, and waved their bows. But as the mass of horsemen moved rapidly away, they ran out in search of prisoners, and Hugh let them go. There was no danger now, and ten minutes later the English knights came trotting back, bascinets open, waving swords and lances, and with them a large batch of prisoners. It had been a well-planned and very successful little skirmish, and the Earl and Sir John were smiling broadly.

'That was well done, Master Hugh,' the Earl said. 'Yes, John, I will come with you to the King, and speak about this.'

There was no point in marching farther into the forest, and the column fell in on the road, and returned to Crécy. The English there were still clearing the battlefield, and loading the wagons with an immense haul of armour and mail. At the baggage park Hugh found Geoffrey, and heard that the army would march north for the coast the next morning.

'Master Fletcher! Master Fletcher!' It was Sir John's squire. 'Sir John would speak to you immediately. I will take you to him.'

Hugh put down his bow and followed the squire, who made for the mill where the King had set up his headquarters. A group of noblemen stood on the grass there, and as he approached, Hugh saw the tall figure of the King, and the Earl of Northampton by his side.

'Hugh!' It was Sir John Carey, and he was smiling. He put his hand on Hugh's shoulder. 'The King has sent for you.'

He pushed Hugh forward, and the noblemen drew aside. Hugh halted and shuffled his feet as he saw the King look up and beckon him.

'We are all much in your debt, young man,' he said. 'Harry, my sword.'

Sir John's hand pressed Hugh again. 'Kneel, boy, kneel!'

Hugh hesitated, and glanced appealingly at Sir John, who nodded and smiled. Clumsily he went down on one knee. The King's sword tapped him lightly.

'Rise, Sir Hugh.'

Hugh gulped and stood up, bewildered and flushing with embarrassment. He saw the young Prince of Wales smiling at him in a friendly manner, and the Earl nodding emphatically. He bowed and stammered his thanks, and backed away, Sir John still holding his arm.

'Here is your first present, Sir Hugh,' he said. 'They are mine, but I should be pleased to see them on you.'

He held out a pair of golden spurs.

HISTORICAL NOTE

The long-bow came into use in England and Wales during the thirteenth and fourteenth centuries, and was so called because it was much longer than any other type of bow. The extra length, measured to fit the height of the bowman, gave great initial velocity, and a range of about three hundred yards. The smooth war-head would penetrate armour and drive into more than four inches of tough wood. The modern archer draws to the mouth, and aims along the line of the shaft, but the medieval bowman drew to the ear, and could loose with an astonishing speed and accuracy.

But the long-bow was an exhausting weapon to draw, and called for years of practice and training before it could be used effectively. This is perhaps the main reason why it gave way in the sixteenth century to the clumsy and slow-firing matchlock musket, which a recruit could be trained to use in a short time. But in the hands of an expert, the long-bow was not surpassed for accuracy and speed of fire until the invention of the magazine loading rifle in the nineteenth century.

The man who actually led the vanguard of the bowmen across the ford at Blanchetaque was Hugh le Despenser, whose tomb can be seen in Tewkesbury Abbey. The course of the Somme has changed so much that it is impossible to say now where the crossing took place, but there is no difficulty in placing the battle of Crécy. The ground has not been built over, and you can stand on the ridge where King Edward drew up his knights and bowmen, and look across the shallow valley to the French positions.

The flight of crows and the thunderstorm before the battle are described by contemporary writers. Historians disagree about the numbers and casualties in the battle, but probably the French had over ten thousand dead out of an army of about forty thousand. The English army was somewhere between ten and fifteen thousand, and their casualties were very few.

There are castles at Goodrich, Grosmont and Skenfrith, all

three just to the north of Monmouth. But I have merely borrowed their names, and have not followed their real plans and buildings. Goodrich is the largest, and is well worth a visit. I have invented the forest of Goodrich, and all the characters in the story, except for such people as King Edward and the Black Prince, and of course, Gobin Agace, though not much is known about him.